ROOM TWENTY-TWO

HIDE AND SEEK

MILA CRAWFORD

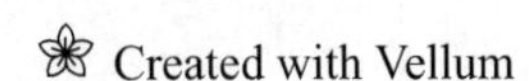
Created with Vellum

AUTHOR'S NOTES

Please be advised this book has a content warning. If you are a sensitive reader please proceed with caution.

Praise. Somnophilia. Degradation. Impact play.Step-brother (One MMC), Primal. Swords Cross. DVP, DP. Red Wings. Period sex. Air tight. Spit Play. Food play. Pegging. Breath play. Marking. Biting.Cream pie clean up.

CNC

Play with red human fluid.

Play with Sharpe objects used to cut meat, fruits and vegetables.

SA on page not of FMC or MMC

Depictions of violence and violent acts (All the MMC are criminals)

STAY CONNECTED

Website

Amazon

TikTok

Facebook

Instagram

GoodReads

The sound of crushing bones and Kevin's screams echoes in the warehouse as Kian pushes the heel of his boot into Kevin's hand. "Too late, Kev. Too fuckin' late."

"Fuck. Why do y'all care anyway? She's just a fat bitch. She'll probably fuck all of you without even blinking. You think I'm the only guy she's banged?"

It happens so fast I don't realize what Ronan's done until a small pool of blood appears around Kevin's crotch.

Kian's the one I would have put my money on shoving a knife into someone's scrotum. Ronan never loses his cool. He never appears to give a damn about anyone or anything. He's funny and charming—he has to be since his dad's a world-famous business tycoon and his mother is the most famous face of Bollywood. So seeing Ronan act like an animal is shocking.

"What the fuck?" Kevin screams.

Ronan smirks as he completely detaches Kevin's dick. "That's the problem, Kevin. You fucked someone who belongs to us. We warned you, and you didn't listen. Since you touched someone who belongs to us, I took what belongs to you."

Kevin holds his crotch with one hand in a pathetic attempt to salvage his severed appendage. “You cut off my dick. All I did was fuck some whore.”

Kian whips the knife from Ronan’s hand. The sound of pierced flesh punctuates the air as Kian thrusts the knife under Kevin’s chin until the tip is visible at the top of his head.

“Why did you have to ruin all our fun?” Ronan demands, shaking his head.

Blood drips from Kevin’s chin as Kian pulls the blade out of his head and shoves it back in. Again and again. “He needed to shut the fuck up.”

A frustrated Ronan throws his hands in the air and growls, “Better call the cleaners.” He turns to me. “She’s gonna think he ditched her.”

“Good. She’ll be licking her wounds, and we don’t have to worry about another fucker touching her,” Kian mumbles.

“You’re a fuckin’ dick, you know that? She’s gonna be hard on herself. You see how she fuckin’ walks around, trying to be invisible. The girl doesn’t even know how fucked up we are over her. She’s gonna take this hard, and all you're worried about is her not looking at another guy. You're a fuckin' dick, Kian."

Kian shrugs. "Never said I wasn't. Facts are facts. If she's crying into her pillow at night, she isn't suckin' another guy's dick."

I hate that a part of me agrees with Kian. She isn't ready for us, and as much as I'd kill a million people for her, I don't want to leave a trail of dead bodies in my wake and tip off my father. The man might be a ruthless killer, but he's never given enough of a fuck about anyone to risk getting his hands dirty for them.

Ronan pulls out one of the white handkerchiefs he always carries. "Let's call the cleaners and get the fuck out of here."

I pull out my phone and dial the number Ronan's father so generously gave us during our high school graduation. Ronan's dad might have more money than God and all the connections of the devil, but eventually, he'll get sick of having to clean up Ronan's mess. The guy might not kill on the daily, but he's a magnet for scandal.

"One day, your dad's gonna cut off that never-ending money tap," I tell him.

Ronan smirks. "Nah, my mom won't let

him. The man loves her so much he'd slit his own throat if she asked him."

Kian paces back and forth, holding the bloody knife in his hand, his face flushed with venom. "What are we gonna do about her?"

"Wait," I say. "We wait for her."

1

Four Years Ago

STELLA

"You gonna drink or sit there looking like a fish out of water?" Annie, a girl I met during rush week, asks.

I gaze at her and then at myself. We couldn't be more different. She's thin, blonde, giggles in all the right places when a guy talks to her and shows more skin than any other girl in the bar. It's no shock that all the guys in the bar are trailing her like pathetic dogs.

I gaze at my jeans and long-sleeved v-neck t-shirt. I must look like a bag of potatoes. "I'm okay with my pop, thanks."

Annie knocks back what must be her tenth blow job. "Suit yourself, girl, but I'm gonna turn up." She grabs the hand of some muscular football player-looking guy and shakes her ass to the dance floor.

I have no clue why I came here. Just like the idea of me rushing for a sorority seems beyond odd. I'm not into this, not into people, dancing, and being surrounded by gyrating bodies humping on a dance floor.

"I get it. It's too much for me, too," a deep voice says beside me.

I turn and come face to face with a handsome guy with sandy hair, dark eyes, and a soft smile. He's wearing glasses, a button-down shirt with the sleeves rolled up to the elbow, and dark denim jeans.

"I don't do people well," I say, staring into my drink.

He smiles. "Maybe we not do people well together?"

I shrug. "If you want."

"Why wouldn't I? You're the prettiest girl in the room."

His words shock me. No one in my entire life has ever said I was pretty, let alone the prettiest girl in a room.

"So, which sorority are you rushing?" he asks.

"None. It's not for me."

"Too bad. I thought I'd see you at more parties. Guess I'll have to impress the shit out of you so you'll agree to dinner with me."

My fingers play with a loose strand of my hair, a nervous habit. I'm so pathetic I don't know what to say. The only guy I've ever dated disappeared as soon as we had sex, so my score card when it comes to the opposite sex is pretty pathetic.

"My name is Bryce, by the way. Hey, I need another drink. Whatcha having?"

"My name is Stella, and I'm good, Bryce, thank you."

"Stella. Such a beautiful name. But I would be a horrible gentleman if I got myself something and not you. My mother would be disappointed. You don't want me to bring disgrace to my mother, do you?'

"I'll have a coke. A virgin, please."

"You got it."

AXEL

What's she doing talking to that guy? I should go up there and beat the shit out of him, but the guys and I agreed we wouldn't mess with her life, at least not to where she'd notice. But if the fucker lays a hand on her, I'll make him bleed.

So I sit back and watch like a motherfuckin' hawk.

They've been talking for over an hour. What the fuck does she have to talk to that dweeb about? He looks like he walked out of a gap commercial. I hate preppy guys. They're usually the biggest dicks. They look all prim and proper, so people give them a pass. He's the fucker who gets away with shit, but society says, "Oh, he didn't know better. Give him another chance." I don't give chances, especially when it comes to her.

They're getting up. The fucker's hand is on her back. I'm going to break that hand and every other fuckin' bone in his body. Crush them under my foot.

I jump up and follow them out the door to his BMW. She's not walking straight. He's holding her up. What the fuck is she doing getting in the car with that guy? And I thought she didn't drink? Why can't she walk?

Motherfucker!

He's got her pressed up against the car. He doesn't see me rush toward him until my fist connects with the side of his face.

"What the—"

I don't let him finish his sentence. I pound him in the face until blood pools on the ground. "You like drugging girls? Raping them?"

"It's not rape. She wants it!" he yells.

"Shut up, asshole." I rip off my belt and tie his hands behind his head. My eyes search the area, looking for something I can use as a gag. I move down his body, taking off one shoe and removing his sock. This should do it.

I move back up his body, forcing his mouth open by plugging up his nose and jamming the dirty sock in his mouth. I don't need him screaming in a dark parking lot. Not that anyone would notice. The place where he parked is secluded, away from everyone. Fucker knew what he was doing. He's obviously done this before.

A bottle of bud light rolls on the ground by his feet. I reach for it, showing it to the fucker. His eyes go wide as I hold it by the neck and smash the bottom.

I unzip his pants and turn him around roughly. "I'm gonna show you what it's like when someone wants it."

He screams as I ram the bottle in his ass. Blood flows and spurts. I'm not gentle. I fuck him over and over and over with the bottle. You want to rape a woman, motherfucker? I'm gonna show you what rape feels like. I fuck him over and over. Pieces of glass from the bottle are lodged up his ass. Tears stream down his pathetic face.

"Don't cry. I'll only make it hurt more. You didn't give a shit about her choice, so I don't give a shit about yours."

Normally I'd put a bullet in his brain and be

done with it, but this motherfucker needs a lesson. I pull the bottle out and smile at him before dragging it along his jugular and watching him bleed out. "Go to hell, motherfucker."

I reach for my phone and call Ronan. "I need a cleanup, now. It's a bar, so call the right people. I can't stick around. I've got to take care of shit."

"What's happening?" Stella mumbles.

She's sitting on the ground, dazed. There's no recognition in her eyes. She has no clue who this guy is. She's in her own world. I'm going to get a security detail on her starting tomorrow. I want to be with her all the time, but my job won't allow it, and I need to know she's safe.

I pick her up, and she holds on to me as if she's meant to be in my arms. "One day soon, Kitten. One day soon, you'll never be away from me."

My feet hit the ground and I run to my car, opening the passenger side door and placing her inside. I lean over and take in her scent as I buckle her in and drive to her small apartment.

2

Four years ago

KIAN

All I have is my art. And my art has taken a different turn. Everything I paint now is of her. Even the abstract work is her in some form. Paintings of her hair, sketches of her eyes, doodles of her lips, brush strokes of her shoulders.

She's the tattoo etched in my brain, taking up all the space and dimming everything else out of focus.

I stare at the painting in front of me, an acrylic piece I've been working on for days. Stella. It's always Stella. Frustration bursts in every cell of my body. A scream escapes my mouth as I take a palette knife to the canvas, cutting it from the top right corner to the bottom left, slashing it in half.

Remorse floods me when I see the slash cutting across her face, and I'm upset at myself for hurting her.

I realize it's a ludicrous thought. It's just a painting. I'd never intentionally hurt a hair on her head. But I know I can destroy her because deep down, a darkness has taken hold of me, and it's always lurking, waiting to take control.

I gaze at the now destroyed image of her face. Emptiness fills me, knowing I've taken something beautiful and made it ugly because I can't control the rage and anger festering inside me.

I gaze at the Chicago skyline through the window. What is she doing? What is she wearing? Who is she with? I sip my bourbon.

Alcohol is the only thing that calms my nerves. I gaze at the auburn liquid in the glass. A pitiful replacement for her.

A few weeks ago, we had to scare off another guy. I hate other men looking at her because they think she's beautiful. I hate how they stare at her curves and tits and want to bury themselves in her. I loathe how she makes their cocks as hard as she makes mine. Jealousy is a poison in my veins bubbling, boiling, and ready to explode.

I want to lock her away like Rapunzel, so no one else can see her but us.

"What the fuck, Kian?" Ronan blares into my room.

I don't realize what's going on until he takes my hand, and I see the blood trickling onto the hardwood floor. I'm glad I insisted on hardwood for my room instead of carpet. Blood stains are a bitch to remove from gray carpet.

Ronan picks shards of glass from my hand. It doesn't hurt. Nothing hurts like the void in my heart from her absence. Being without her is the most painful loss imaginable.

"You gotta stop doing this, man. It's only a

couple more years. We can't lose you as soon as we get her, Kian. You gotta stay strong," Ronan says.

"She's so far away. Why couldn't she have gone to school here? She should've stayed in Chicago. We should've made her stay here."

I'm in such a daze that I don't register Ronan walking me to the bathroom faucet. I'm a mindless zombie, unaware of what's happening from one moment to another.

Ronan runs my hand under the cold water. The crimson blends with the clear liquid. "She's too young, Kian. We did this so she'd have time. She needs to stand toe to toe with us. We aren't normal guys. We're too much in every way. She needs to live. She has to know not to fear us, to take us on. We did what was best for her. We need to be patient. Two more years, and she's ours. All ours. Forever. Two more years, and we'll all be together."

I dig the heel of my uninjured hand in my eye. "I can't do it. She's fuckin' everywhere I look. She's all I think about, all I want. I can't do it."

Ronan drops my hand, turning to face me.

He grabs my face before connecting his forehead to mine. "You gotta get yourself under control, man. You gotta pull yourself together because it only works if it's the four of us. Axel and I cannot lose you. You gotta be strong. I need her too, Kian. I fucking need her too."

3

Two Years later

AXEL

"You've gotta calm down with this trophy bullshit," Ronan says as he shuffles through a wooden box full of mementos I've taken from her over the years. I didn't mean to be a bona fide stalker. I miss her.

When she was a senior in high school, I saw her every day and got my fill of her beauty. But then she moved to Boston, and everything changed. I couldn't drive to the school and stare at her as she took pictures of the football game for the school paper or follow her on the Loop on her way home.

So I started flying to Boston every weekend. I followed her on campus and did background checks on everyone she spoke to. Eventually, it escalated to breaking into her small bachelor apartment.

At first, I stared at her while she slept. It gave me a sense of calm, knowing she was safe. But I needed more—much more—so I started stealing her things, minor items she wouldn't notice but brought me the desperate sense of peace I needed.

"Between you and Kian, I'm gonna lose my fuckin' mind. He's turned into a quivering mess, and you've turned into some sort of psycho stalker," Ronan says in disgust.

I lift my head off his cock and gaze up at him. "You're gonna get on my case about a change of behavior? You're a fuckin whore and the only person sucking your dick lately is me."

"We've been sucking each other off since high school. She's got nothing to do with my cock being lodged up your throat," Ronan shoots back. "A warm mouth is a warm mouth. Besides, I trust your ass with my life, but I don't trust random chicks with shit."

"You trust her," I point out.

"Yes, I fuckin' trust her. I don't have any logic about why. But giving up pussy was easy because I can't even think about sticking it to someone else."

I sit on the couch beside Ronan and tilt my head back, staring at the patterns on the ceiling. Why did anyone think it was a good idea to have elaborate designs where no one sees them?

I rub my eyes. Ronan's right. We've been fucking each other since high school. We never shared a girl, not with all three of us. Sure, we'd occasionally have a threesome here or there, a tag team, or a spit roast. And all the girls we've had a threesome with never lasted more than a night. They were novelties, never anything more.

But not Stella. Not once have all three of us wanted to share a girl. Not until her. She's gotten under our skin, imprinted herself in our minds, and stolen our hearts. Stella is the woman we've been looking for. The missing link. The heart that binds us.

"I get it, man. I don't want another girl either. Shit, I'd give up you and Kian if it meant I could have her. Never thought I'd say that. I don't know why I keep going back to her apartment and taking her shit. It's the quickest way to get busted. Sometimes I sit by her bed and watch her sleep like a fucking psycho. I know I'm messed up in the head, but I never thought I'd be so stuck on a woman. But fuck… It's like I need to be near her to breathe. How the fuck aren't you going crazy, Ronan?"

"I keep telling myself it's only two more years. In two years, she's ours, and it's over."

I get up from the couch, walk to my dresser and open the top drawer. As soon as I touch the panties, my cock twitches. I turn around and dangle the piece of cotton in front of Ronan's face. "Stole these. I have seven pairs of her panties, three of them used." I bring the underwear to my nostrils and sniff. "It's kind of fucked up. This is the only thing I have of hers in the last few years, underwear stained with her scent. I lie in bed like a depraved maniac, inhaling or licking them while I jerk off, picturing her mouth wrapped around my cock."

Ronan rips the panties from my hand and sniffs them. "Jerk my cock."

I move my hand to his dick, moving it up and down his thick shaft. "I want to tag team her. Fill up all her holes. God, can you imagine how tight her pussy and ass will be? How hot she'll look dripping our cum from each of her holes?"

"I want to come with you next time," Ronan says. "While she sleeps, I want to touch her pussy. I need to sniff that sweet cunt from the source."

"We can fly out tonight. I can suck your cock while you smell her. Fuck, that's hot."

"Stop jerking me! I want to blow a giant load into her panties." Ronan rises off the couch and pulls out his phone. "Get the jet ready. Now!"

"How the fuck do you have a key to her place?" Ronan asks.

I unlock and open the door slowly. "Keep your voice down. I don't want anyone else seeing us sneaking in. I've got connections in Boston. They know the owner of the building. People rarely say no to the mob when their lives are at risk."

"Fuck, this place is a closet," Ronan says as he gazes at the small space. A bed against one wall, a small kitchen with a mini-fridge, and a tiny stove in the corner. A door that opens to a small washroom. "Jesus, we can't let her live here. How is this hell hole not a health violation?"

"I got her a scholarship," I remind him. "She put the money in the bank. I worked out another one. Part of it is an apartment. She's stubborn."

Ronan chuckles. "You like it. You've got a thing for brats."

"Yeah, when I'm fuckin' them. I don't want this shit when I'm doing what's good for her."

4

Four Years Ago

RONAN

I'm a sick fuck. I realize how wrong this is, but I don't give a damn. Because at this moment, as I stand by her bed, staring down at her raven hair fanned around her face, I don't care how perverted I am.

All I want is to curl up in that bed and fuck her until she's so spent she can't think straight.

Her mouth is slightly parted. There are no covers on her curvy frame. Her thick legs are bare, her nipples poke through her thin baseball jersey, and the outline of her pussy is visible through her thin cotton panties. My cock's rock hard just looking at her. "She's so fuckin' beautiful."

"Yes, she is," Axel whispers.

My mouth waters as I think about taking her pert nipples between my lips.

Axel's hand moves to my crotch. He tugs at the zipper of my pants and frees my cock. "Spit on my hand, Ronan," he demands.

I spit on his hand before licking it, making it nice and wet. Axel tugs at my cock and milks a moan from my lips.

"I want to eat her pussy out right now," Axel whispers in my ear. "You could fuck her pussy while I eat her out. Kian would take her ass, and we'd make her nice and tight. Then, when you're both ready to blow your load, I tug her hair, get her on her knees, and cum on her beautiful face. She'll be so hot covered in our cum, our perfect little fuck doll. We'll stare at her, admiring how she looks claimed by us before we lick the cum, tasting each other off her face. When she's ours, I'm gonna pound that pussy so hard she'll be sore for weeks."

"If you keep talking like that, I'm gonna cum all over your hand," I grunt.

I remove Axel's hand from my cock and walk to the end of the bed. I kneel and crawl onto the bed, making sure not to wake her. My eyes zone in on her cotton-covered pussy. I bring my nose right up to her cunt and sniff.

Fuck, she smells good.

For Stella, I am a recovering addict. Able to abandon all drugs and go without until I'm face to face with the drug of my choice. Giving up women for the past few years has been easy. I'm not tempted to look at them, let alone fuck them, but face to cunt with Stella, I'm desperate to get high on her.

I should be more careful. I'm being too bold, and I know it. She could wake up at any moment, freak out, and never want anything to do with us again. What I'm doing could cause us to lose her forever, but like an addict, I can't think about the repercussions. I just want the hit.

My body shakes at the idea of touching her. My mouth waters with the burning desire to bury my tongue in her hot cunt. I want to feel her, smell her, devour her, be consumed by her scent, and drown in her beauty. I don't know what she's done to me or the spell she's conjured, but I know I'm hers in every way and always will be.

My balls are heavy with need, and my cock is as hard as steel. Axel's warm mouth engulfs the tip of my shaft, and my hips dip until I hit the back of his throat. I close my eyes and picture Stella choking on my fat dick.

His tongue wraps around my shaft. The torturous swipe along the head of my cock is enough to drive me insane. I groan into her pussy, and she moans, opening her legs wider, exposing more of her sweetness to my hungry gaze.

My fingers twitch and shake as I gently tug, pulling her panties to the side, careful not to wake her. I desperately try not to touch her, but the tip of my index finger has a mind of its own. It brushes a feather touch on her engorged clit. She's so wet. So ready. I could take her right now and fill her with my cum.

Axel's hand plays with my balls as his mouth milks over my cock. The sensation of being so near her cunt is too much to bear. I pull my cock out of Axel's mouth and line myself up against Stella's pussy. I pump my cock a few times and blow right onto her cotton panties. Knowing she'll wake up in the morning with my cum on her panties is so fucking erotic. She'll have my scent on her.

Mine.

5

Present Day

STELLA

My foot hits the pavement as I get out of the ostentatious limo my new stepfather sent to the airport for me. I told my mom I'd be fine taking a cab like your average college student, but my new stepfather, Anthony Moretti, can't have his trophy wife's daughter traveling as a common peasant.

I glance up at the mausoleum that's supposed to be a home. A medieval-style castle right in the middle of a Chicago suburb. Stones layered on each other with large turrets and actual gargoyle statues in the middle of a lush forest full of European buckthorns, green ash, and American Elm. The structure is a far cry from the one-bedroom apartment my mother and I lived in when I was in high school. Looks like I'm not in Kansas anymore.

The driver stands beside me, bags in hand as if waiting for an order. As if I can tell anyone what to do.

"I can take those." I reach out to grab my two bags.

He quickly pulls his arms away. "No, Miss. That's not how it works. I walk you to the front door and discard your bags there."

I want to argue. I'm not used to this. Rich people have a completely different standard of living than us commoners. I nod and walk up the stone steps to the massive oak doors with the giant lion knocker. The driver opens the door and waits, not saying a word. He stands there with his arms to his sides and my bags by his feet.

"Oh, there you are, Miss Stella," a dark-haired woman in a business suit and tight bun says. She nods at the driver, who returns her nod and leaves. "My name is Heidi." She juts her hand out, and I shake it. "I'm the manor's executive assistant. It's lovely to meet you."

"It's nice to meet you."

"Mr. Moretti and your mother have been called away on business. They've informed me they'll be back in two days. Should I show you to your room?"

I nod. "That would be great, thank you."

I move to grab my bags, but Heidi's firm hand stops me. "Please, leave those. We will bring them up to your room."

I shake off her hand and take hold of my bags. "No, it's okay. I'd rather take them up with me now. Lead the way."

Heidi gives me a disappointed stare, her lips set in a firm line. Nodding briskly, she walks us to a large marble staircase. I can't help wondering if my new stepfather has more money than God. Who has a marble staircase?

"We've put you in this room," Heidi says,

opening French doors into what looks like a five thousand-a-night hotel room, complete with eight-hundred count Egyptian cotton sheets and high vaulted ceilings. “Mr. Axel is across the hall. He’s Mr. Moretti’s son. He’s around your age, maybe a few years older.”

I’m familiar with Axel Moretti. We went to the same high school. I was a freshman when he was a senior.

Being a smart poor kid, I got scholarships to prestigious schools my entire life, passing any test they threw at me with flying colors. I begged my mom not to force me to go to a school where I stood out like a sore thumb. She simply smiled and told me it was for my future, and an education was the only thing that would ensure I didn’t end up like her. I never thought there was anything wrong with being like her. My mom worked hard at two server jobs to keep us off the streets after my dad died of cancer, leaving us completely alone in the world. Her parents abandoned us, treating us like strangers because she married a man they disapproved of. My mom didn’t want me to struggle like she did, so all the begging in the world wouldn’t make her budge.

I learned to keep myself invisible at these schools, hidden so no one paid any attention to me. If they can't see you, they won't bother you. That was my motto throughout my life. Because the truth is, Axel and I might as well be from different planets.

I'd noticed Axel and his two arrogant best friends. All attractive, all filthy rich kings of the school. What they said went, and if you messed with them, you would hear about it, probably with their fists and boots.

In high school, I remember walking into the girls' locker room my senior year and witnessing Axel, Ronan, and Kian beating the shit out of a guy for God knows what. I remember thinking it was odd that it took place in the girls' locker room, but I was too petrified to say anything. If I spoke, I wouldn't be invisible anymore, and that wasn't something I could afford. I didn't have their connections, their money, or their good looks. I was the fat, poor girl while they were royalty, sitting high on their untouchable thrones.

They went in on him like jackals ripping apart their prey. And the look of complete and utter annihilation on Axel's face was the scariest thing I'd ever seen. So I've avoided the man like the plague since our parents started dating.

I walked into the "help" he gives people, and it's not something I'm interested in. Sure, he's as hot as sin, but his heart is as dark as coal.

Heidi plasters a forced smile on her face as she backs out of the bedroom and closes the French doors behind her, leaving me alone. My hand glides along the bed and my brain goes into overdrive. What has my mother gotten us into? She might have all these extravagant things, but at what cost? The Morettis aren't exactly upstanding citizens. One of the most notorious mobsters in the Midwest and the constant source of fame in the tabloids. The one most in the tabloids is Anthony's playboy son, Axel. Not that Axel is a harmless frat boy. He's got a reputation for being lethal and someone you don't want to mess with.

The giant room suddenly feels too small, making it hard to breathe. I fling the bedroom doors open and storm into the hallway. Bending over so my head is level with my knees, I breathe deeply, desperate to calm myself down. I should be excited to be living in a place as luxurious as this, but all I want is my small chair by the window and the cramped walls of our one-bedroom in our old, rundown neighborhood.

The silence here is eerie. It's so quiet that it's deafening. How the hell can anyone sleep without car alarms erupting in the middle of the night or the blare of a police siren?

My eyes flutter shut as I center myself. The last thing I need is to go into a full-blown panic attack in strange surroundings. I breathe slowly and gently before exhaling and counting. Over the years, I've learned to breathe, try to find a calming thought and talk myself off the ledge. The counting helps me focus. It lets me know I'm in control and I've got this.

I pull myself up and grab the banister. I'm about to head outside and see if fresh air can help when I hear a grunt from the room across the hall.

I should mind my business and go outside like I'd planned, but a morbid curiosity takes hold of me, and my feet glide along the marble floor. The door is ajar, and like a complete creeper, I place my eye between the crack of the door and the door frame and peek inside.

That's when I see my new step-brother, Axel Moretti, his head tilted back on a black leather couch, his arms expanding like an eagle. His crisp white dress shirt is open, and my eyes trail along his firm chest and banging six-pack. I see a head bopping up and down between his legs. Axel's getting a blow job, and like some pervert, I'm watching.

"Fuck,' Axel moans.

Wetness pools between my legs as if he swiped my clit with his tongue. I don't know why I'm mesmerized by the scene, but here I am, completely turned on.

"I need to get laid by a chick cause as much as it's hot fuckin' around with the two of you, it'll never compare to a wet, warm pussy."

My eyes shift to the fresh voice, and there sits Kian, the psycho.

Axel and Ronan are insane, but they're nothing compared to Kian. When I saw them attack that guy at my school, it was Kian who relished it. It took me months to get his face drenched in crimson out of my mind. The more blood he saw, the more he attacked the poor guy. It was as if the color red had fueled him. Ronan seemed to be the least insane, but even he had no issues taking a crowbar to the guy's knees and shattering them.

Kian's hand moves back and forth around his thick cock, and what a dick it is. I've seen a couple of cocks in my lifetime, but none as beautiful as the one Kian is sporting. Even from here, I can see it's a work of art.

Axel grunts, and the sound is so primal it goes straight to my clit. I forget these three men are psychopaths with no humanity and think about how wet I am. I'm not the type to spy on people, but something about seeing these men in a compromising position does all kinds of things to my body.

My hand moves to my breasts and I fist them in my hand while the other hand moves under my dress and glides into my panties. Every grunt and groan coming from these men is a hit directly on my clit. My eyes close as my fingers work me into a frenzy. I'm lost in their euphoria while trying to find my own when I hear a thud. My eyes fly open to see Ronan on his ass, Kian putting his dick away, and Axel looking at me like he'd like to set me on fire.

"Christ, Axel. You could give a man warning," Ronan says.

"Look what we have here," Axel says, walking over to me. He's not even trying to hide his bobbing erection. His massive biceps bulge. "Little Kitten, I think the big bad wolves have caught you."

I try to remove my hand from my panties, but Axel is quicker. He holds me in position and steps closer. My body shakes, not from the orgasm I was hoping to have but from the venom in his clear blue eyes. "We don't like curious little kittens around here. Think we need to punish you, so you know your place?"

I try to find my courage. "I'm sure Daddy would like to know about your little display here." I shake my wrist, but his grip is like a vise. "Let go of my arm, Axel."

"It's cute she thinks she can tell you what to do," Ronan says, his voice laced with something akin to respect.

My eyes roam to the side, and I spot Kian, a hunting knife in his hand. "I say we teach someone some manners."

Axel smirks. "Is that what we should do, Little Kitten? Teach you some manners."

I swallow, my body a tense ball of nerves. I've walked into a den of lions.

A laughing bark jolts my fear. I turn to stare Ronan in the face. His smile is jovial, his eyes pierced on mine as he zips his pants. "What's the matter, Rabbit? Not feeling brave anymore?"

"Let's make a deal, Little Kitten. You run, and we chase. If we don't catch you, all's forgiven, and we all go about our merry way."

"And what happens if you catch me?'

Kian's deep voice reverberates through the room. "Then we have a little fun." He licks his lips while trailing the blade of the knife on the couch cushion. "Our way."

"Don't waste any time, Kitten. You've got a ten-minute head start." Axel leans in, his mouth at my ear. His breath is hot, and my body, the slut it is, doesn't seem to care he's crazy. It takes a moment before he whispers the word, "Run."

6

AXEL

The kitten scampers down the stairs. Kian laughs. The sick fuck might be my brother, but I'm sure he's salivating at catching her as much as I am. I'm sick, too, but I'm no match for Kian. The guy has no control; everything is about access to him. It's as if the only time he can feel is when he's too far gone.

Kian moves the tip of his blade along his fingertip. "How long we gonna let her run?"

"You can put that away cause you're not

using it on her," I instruct. I've seen Kian at work with that knife, with the look of pure exaltation when he draws blood. In a twisted way, it's like he takes their life force and seeps it into himself. It's the only time he doesn't seem like the fuckin' walking undead.

Kian laughs and tosses the knife on the marble coffee table, tip down. "No problem. There are a lot of other things I can do with Sweet Girl that won't require cutting."

"You can't force her into shit either," Ronan chirps. Of the three of us, Ronan is the only one with some humanity. It's not much, but it's there. He gazes at me, his brown eyes giving off a disapproving stare.

"You want to fuck her too," I throw back, and he looks away, proving me right.

We all wanted to bang her when we saw her in the form-fitting dress at my dad's wedding to her mom. How she looked in that dress is still imprinted on my mind, every luscious curve hugged tight. I wanted to push her against the wall and grope every fuckin' part of her. She consumed me at the wedding, and I couldn't pay attention to anything but her. She kept tugging at her dress as if she was uncomfortable, like she had no idea how fuckin' hot she was. My mouth watered as I stared at her giant tits overflowing the top of her dress.

I tried to talk to her at the wedding, but every time she saw me approach, she ran like I petrified her. Later, I found out she'd spotted us beating up a football player in our senior year of high school. She didn't know why we kicked the shit out of him until he was gasping for his final breaths, but we had reasons, good ones.

From that day she became the only thing we craved, and nothing we did could make it go away.

Kian's art took a very dark and obsessive turn. Ronan stopped fucking everything that walked, and I started stalking her, taking little mementos where I could. Like an addict, I fly to her campus every week and watch her for a few days, needing the hit to take the edge off.

One of the reasons we started fuckin' around with each other was to get some relief from our obsession with her because no other woman would do once she crawled deep under our skin. We care about each other, so it's not like we're completely using one another to get our rocks off. Sexuality is a fucked-up construct, but I can confidently say Stella is the pinnacle for all of us.

It's probably wrong that when we catch her, we're going to take what we want without remorse, but it's her fault for getting into our bloodstream like a fuckin' virus.

"Fuckin' her won't keep her under control, and it won't make her ours," Ronan says. "You know what we've gotta do."

I nod.

Kian smirks as he rolls up his sleeves. "Don't worry. We'll make her a quiet and willing little toy."

"Ready?" I ask.

The guys nod, and we walk down the stairs and out the back doors, watching Stella run amongst the trees.

We catch up to her in no time; her strides are no match for ours. "You can run, but you'll never be able to hide."

She turns around, tripping on a rock and falling to her knees. She gathers herself and starts to run, but I grab her by the waist and pull her toward me. "I like you in that position, Kitten. You look mighty fine on your knees, like a good girl."

She struggles to get away, pushing her fat ass against my cock, making it hard as fuck. She doesn't seem to understand that the more she struggles, the more I want her. My hands roam her body, and I grab her tits. Shock runs through me as I rub her pebbled nipples. "The chase turn you on?"

"No!" she yells.

I push her toward a tree, my body covering hers like a blanket. She inhales when I press my cock against her, making her feel every fuckin' inch of me. My hand climbs to her throat, and I press my fingers into her jugular. Her eyes go round, and her fear is so palatable I could drown in it. "What's the matter, sweetheart? You like watching from the sidelines, but you don't want to take part in the game?"

I trail my free hand down her body, stopping at her giant tits. Her fuckin' tits. They are a goddamn work of art. Perfect, perky, and massive. I grab a handful of her decadent flesh and dig my fingers in. "These tits have haunted my dreams."

Her breath hitches, but she doesn't fight me. Disappointing, although my throbbing cock doesn't give a fuck. I skim my nose along her neck, trailing up to her ear. I growl my frustration and need before I suck her delicate flesh so hard I know I'll be leaving my mark.

Good. I want her to walk around with my scent and bruises on her, to feel me for days. She's at my mercy. Mine.

Abandoning her breasts, my hand slides down her flesh. I caress every luscious curve of her body, gliding to the hem of her dress and fisting the material to expose her creamy thighs.

She flinches as my hand travels on her bare skin. My fingers slip into her panties, and I'm greeted with her slickness as my other hand laces through her dark hair and tugs her head back. My eyes lock with hers, and I smirk. "It must be so confusing to want to fuck someone you can't stand."

"Please! I've got… it's my…"

My hand moves to her entrance. We both freeze.

"Kitten, I'm a real man. That won't stop me," I say as I pull her tampon out of her cunt and dangle the blood-covered material in front of her face.

Before she can respond, I discard her

tampon and replace it with not one but two fingers. Removing them from her drenched cunt, I show them to her. Shock flashes across her face as I suck on my fingers, devouring her in my mouth.

"Tastes good, baby. I can't wait to have you sitting on my face like a wanton whore."

She turns her head away when I offer her my fingers. It's cute that she thinks her minor act of defiance will stop me. "I like it rough, sweetheart."

I release her hair and plug her nose, forcing her to open her mouth and shove my fingers from her blood-stained cunt into her mouth. Her eyes flash with venom, but her body melts into my touch as her lips close around my fingers. Slowly, I withdraw them, and a sigh escapes her full lips. "Wasn't too bad, was it?"

"It was horrible. You disgust me."

"Is that so, Kitten?" I move my hand back to her slit and rub her clit, circling it with the tip of my finger. "Your drenched cunt has other ideas. Looks like you're not the perfect little girl mommy and stepdaddy think you are. Your dirty pussy is weeping. It's okay to admit you're a filthy whore." The little kitten might think she wouldn't be into this, but her body is calling her a liar.

"Please," she pleads.

I take my fingers out of her panties and streak her cheek with her blood. "What's the matter, Kitten?"

"Why did you stop touching me?'

I bark out a laugh. "Oh, Kitten. Did you think we'd let you come that easily? Did you think we were here for your pleasure and not ours? How about you get on your knees and show us how badly you're willing to work to come?"

Stella kneels before me without complaining. My foot slides between her knees, pushing them apart. "Such a pretty cock whore."

7

STELLA

The soft soil digs into my knees, grounding me. If I focus on the earth, I'll be able to handle anything they throw at me. Their behavior shouldn't shock me. I know what these three are. It's not like I can do anything to stop them from committing any act of depravity they want to me. I'm simply the peasant while they're royalty, sitting high above on their perch, untouchable.

"You're doing so well, pretty girl," Ronan

says, rubbing his large hand down my hair. His gentle touch is a contrast to Axel's roughness.

I gaze up at him, and his honey-laden eyes don't appear as harsh as Axel's ice-blue ones. Ronan bites his lip, his head bent as if he might regret whatever happens next. His strong hand tangles in my hair as he gently pats me like a parent trying to console a distraught child.

"Beautiful. So damn beautiful. You want to be a good girl for us, don't you?" Ronan's voice is hypnotic, his words addictive.

I shock myself by nodding my head in agreement. I'm not sure why I want to make him happy, but I do. Perhaps it's the sadness I see lurking in his eyes or that, unlike Axel, he's being kind. It's not like these guys are repulsive. Far from it. They're the most handsome men I've ever seen, but the idea of being forced to do something doesn't sit well with me.

Ronan's soft touch and deep voice calm my frazzled nerves, and I don't feel the need to fight like I did ten minutes ago. Gooseflesh pricks at my skin and shivers race up and down my spine as Ronan's fingers trail along my cheek to my neck. His muscular frame looms over me as I gaze up at him. He's larger than life, but he's also comforting. Ronan has mesmerized me into thinking he's some knight in shining armor, but it's a mirage. Ronan, like Axel and Kian, is a monster. This isn't a fairy tale with noble Princes. I have walked into the demon's den

Ronan's lips pull into a slow, seductive smile as he crouches down and brings his cool lips to my sensitive ear. My body ignites when his warm breath hits my skin. "Open up, Rabbit. Show Axel how well you can take his cock in your pretty little mouth."

My lips part as if God has given me an order, and if I don't move quickly enough, he'll strike me down. As much as I want to pretend it's fear making me comply, there's a much stronger allure to these three. The same allure that's been present from the day I saw them in the locker room.

Ronan smiles at me encouragingly, and my body buzzes with desire and thunders with need. The elation is short-lived because soon, the devil himself places the tip of his cock on my lips, smearing them with his pre-cum.

Axel isn't the same as Ronan. He doesn't give off the same sense of calm or protection. His eyes roam my face, and I see the hunger lurking in his eyes. Axel is an animal desperate for the hunt. He's the predator, and I'm simply his pathetic prey.

"Eyes on me, baby doll," Ronan demands.

I shift my vision toward him. His lips turn up as he gives me an approving smile right before Axel shoves his dick down my throat.

"Such a pretty little whore," he grunts as he thrusts into my mouth, fucking it with vigor and force.

He pushes his cock to the back of my throat. I'm losing control, and my worst fear is what this man will do to me if I dare barf on his dick. Axel doesn't seem to care that I'm gagging. It seems to turn him on, which shouldn't shock me since I'm on my knees wearing my period blood on my face, courtesy of him.

His hand fists my throat, constricting my breathing even more. *Oh, God, he's going to kill me.* The knowledge should make me bite down on his steel rod and run, but my pussy is so wet I'm about to hump the forest grounds, hoping to relieve the ache.

"Keep looking at me, pretty girl," Ronan coos.

Ronan, being the smooth talker out of the

three, makes sense. The guys got a reputation with women more infamous than Leonardo DiCaprio. Both rich and beautiful, the son of a Russian Oligarch with rumored ties to the Bratva and one of the most beautiful Bollywood stars to have ever lived.

"That's it, sweetheart," Ronan encourages. "Relax your throat and take him like a good girl. You're making us so happy with your perfect mouth."

Axel and Ronan are both active participants in my degrading sexual awakening, but I spot Kian from the corner of my eye. His brows are furrowed, one strand of his shaggy, black hair falling over his wicked green eyes, his arms crossed as he leans casually against a tree. His gaze is on me, watching the show unfold, but he looks disinterested, almost bored. I don't know why it bothers me to see him like that, but it does. I should be relieved he hasn't touched me, especially knowing what he's capable of, but his distance heightens my insecurity. I don't appreciate the intrusive thoughts rattling in my brain about my weight or the fact that I don't appeal to him. Now I want to kick my ass for putting myself down. I know I'm attractive, but sometimes the bullshit that's taunted me thanks to the fucked-up superficial world we live in weasels into my mind and tries to undermine what I know to be the truth.

Axel doesn't have the same problem as Kian. He presses the back of my head against the trunk of a tree as he continues to assault my throat mercilessly. I gag, desperate for relief, but he doesn't care. The harder I struggle, the more he pushes my boundaries. And as much as I hate to admit it, I'm turned on—more turned on than I've ever been.

"Looks like our kitten has superior cock sucking skills," Axel grunts as he pulls out of my mouth.

I gasp for breath. My head falls forward, and saliva cascades from my open mouth, gliding down my chin and falling on the dirt. My head is yanked back, and I'm forced to gaze directly into Axel's blue eyes while he slaps my face with his hand. "You're so pretty with your mouth open, begging for cock. A perfect little whore for us to use and play with."

I should be furious at how he's talking to me, about being called a whore, but I'm so horny and desperate to come, I'd let him call me anything to get some relief.

I move my head forward, sticking out my tongue as I try to lick the tip of Axel's cock as he holds it away from me. "Please," I beg. I'm so pathetic, but I'll worry about that another day.

Axel taunts me by rubbing the tip of his cock along my lips. "You're so pretty when you're begging to be my cum dumpster."

Humiliation washes over me, but I can't deny his words.

"Take out your tits," Kian's says, pulling me from my trance.

My eyes shift toward his Italian black leather shoes as they crunch the forest debris beneath them. I'm paralyzed, a marionette to be used by my puppet masters.

Kian walks in front of me, and Axel moves out of the way. "You won't like it if I have to tell you again. Be a good girl and do as you're told."

Now isn't the best time to show resistance, but I can't help it. I stay in my current position, ignoring Kian's' demands. My defiance doesn't anger him. Instead, he stands there and smirks at me as if proud of my behavior. His hands gently move through my hair, and I think I've done the right thing until I feel the burn on my scalp. Tears stream down my face, the pain unbearable.

He lifts me by my hair and shoves me onto the cold ground. "Sweet Girl, when I ask you to do something, you better jump. The more you resist, slut, the more I'll hurt you." He grabs my hand and places it on his steel cock. "Hurting you makes me hard as fuck."

Kian tugs my breasts from my dress, exposing me to the eyes of my step-brother and Ronan. "That's better, my little slut." My right breast jiggles as Kian slaps it hard and laughs. "Keep that sexy mouth open. Axel's not done throat fucking you."

I do as I'm told. I've never been this aroused in all my twenty-two years. I've always had to use lubricant to be this wet with other men. My body didn't respond to them. Everything these men are doing, with the exception of Ronan, should elicit fear in me. But the only reaction my body and mind can conjure is lust.

Axel laughs and slaps me across the face with his dick. "I enjoy having you in this position. Knees apart, mouth open, waiting for my cock." He rams his dick into my throat, his eyes rapturous as he gazes at my breasts. "You've got great tits, Kitten. Big and juicy. I can't wait to get a good look at your sweet cunt and see if it's as luscious as your tits. Your body is fuckin' amazing. So fuckin' sexy."

His words are shocking because I've never considered my body amazing. Sure, I have big tits. It's part and parcel of being a size twenty-two, but no one has ever told me my figure is amazing, let alone sexy.

As if sensing my hesitation, Axel grabs my stomach in his hand and pinches, making me flinch. "This is hot. This gets my cock rock hard. You're such a pretty slut, and you don't even know it. Every fuckin' inch of you is a walking wet dream."

Kian steps behind me and grabs my tits, wraps his fingers around my nipples, and tugs hard. "You should have some jewelry on these pretty pink nipples."

My eyes go wide and I mumble a no, but Axel's massive cock lodged in my throat makes my word illegible, and all that comes out is a moan. Or maybe I moaned because being debased by these men makes me lose all sense of sanity.

Axel pinches my nostrils, and Kian twists my nipples so viciously I'm sure I'm going to die on the forest floor, but my pussy seems to think all this is a brilliant idea. People say guys only think with their dicks, but apparently, a woman's vagina is a moron too.

Kian doesn't stop abusing my tits, lifting my breast with one hand while the other twists my nipple harder and harder until I can't take it, and I scream.

Axel groans. "Do it again. When the slut screams, my cock likes it."

Kian bends down and takes my nipple into his mouth. He trails his fingers up my thighs until he's moving in and out of my pussy. His fingers are large, and they feel so good. His tongue moves in circular motions on my nipples, and between his gentle lapping and his fingers on my pussy, I relax.

My body yearns to come, and my mind desperately hopes Kian will finally allow my release. But he squashes my hopes when he takes my nipple between his teeth and bites. Hard. I'm positive when he removes his mouth, my nipple will be lodged between his teeth. My scream is earth-shattering, but it only makes Axel pound harder into my mouth.

Kian smiles, his fingers still deep inside my cunt, his eyes mesmerized by my breasts. “Based on this wet cunt, you like it. Stop pretending you’re anything but our dirty fuckin’ whore. You’re a dirty pain slut too, Stella. I’m going to have a lot of fun with you.”

I look down to see two trickles of blood sliding down my skin and landing on my dress. My eyes go wide as I see the mischievous smirk on Kian’s face. Humiliation rolls over me, knowing they can do whatever they want, and I’ll crave every depraved moment.

KIAN

She's perfect. Never in my life have I seen a woman more stunning than her. Her body is straight out of every fuckin' wet dream I've ever had. The angels carved her face, and now I know she's a little pain slut, she's paradise made flesh.

I've always acknowledged that hurting someone during sex turns me on. That or watching people have rough sex. Maybe that's why I can get it up when I watch my two best friends fuck, and why this situation with Stella has my cock ready to go. The way she takes anything we throw at her like a champ is a turn-on. She'll be able to give us what we need, fight us, push us, and we'll do the same for her. A balance.

She might pretend she doesn't like the pain, but it's a game cause her pussy gushed like fuckin' Niagara Falls. The girl likes it rough. When I almost ripped off her nipple, she practically came on my fingers.

I pull my blood-stained fingers from her sweet cunt and place them in front of her face. Axel moves out of her, and I pull her hair back, shoving my fingers down her throat until I hit her gag reflex. Her eyes are wide, but she doesn't put up a fight. "My little toy. I'm going to have so much fun with you. Such a good little slut licking off your dirty, bloody cunt from my fingers."

Her soft tongue loops around my fingers, and her eyes close as she eagerly cleans herself off my thick digits. I pull them out, and her eyes shoot open. "Why don't you own up to what you are?"

"What am I?" she asks.

"Our filthy slut. Say it, Stella. Tell us exactly what you are."

Fury flashes in her eyes. Defiance. The little minx doesn't know how much of a turn on the fire within her is. From the moment I saw her again standing in the corner at her mother's wedding like a little mouse, desperate to avoid any type of attention, I've been waiting for the perfect moment. She became an obsession. I pictured her big brown eyes and perfectly plump lips every time I closed my eyes at night. And when I finally fell asleep, I dreamt about all the depraved things I'd do to her curvy frame once I got my hands on her.

She isn't responding to my question, but she doesn't seem to understand that in this game, we're the ones who get what we want, not her. At least, not yet. She needs to be broken before she becomes the center of our universe.

Axel grips her jaw, forcing her gaze to him. He hooks the side of her lips, stretching her mouth. "You might not want to admit what you are, but we'll use you like one, anyway."

He plunges his cock between her lips and pushes through. Axel usually has control, but it seems nonexistent with her. He isn't holding back, his need visible as his hips thrust deep into Stella's mouth. He doesn't seem to care that there's a person attached to the throat he's using like a fleshlight. To anyone watching, Stella is nothing but an available hole, there for his pleasure. But she's his obsession, like she's mine and Ronan's.

I lift her head off Axel's cock by her hair. "You better speak up, Sweet Girl. He won't have any mercy unless you do."

Her gaze moves to mine, but she doesn't move, mouth closed, eyes cold. I smile as I wrap my hand around her throat and squeeze. Her pretty brown eyes widen, and horror washes over her face. All I can think about is how hot she looks on the brink of passing out by my hand and how I can't wait to bury my cock deep inside her. "You seem to think you still have control here, sweetheart." A lone tear runs down her face, and I release her, letting her recoil on the ground huddled beside a tree.

I turn to see Axel and Ronan taking off their pants, getting more comfortable as they prepare for the main event.

Ronan approaches her first. He touches her gently, and her eyes shoot up to his. The fear she shows me and the disdain she shows Axel isn't present. For Ronan, she's amiable, like she welcomes his touch. My heart twists. It's confusing. I don't like that she doesn't respond that way to me.

"You want to be a good girl for us, don't you, baby?" Ronan asks, and she nods her head. "You like being treated like our whore, don't you?" She nods again. "Can you tell Kian what you are?"

To my surprise, she nods and says, "I'm your filthy little whore."

Ronan fists his cock, and Stella licks her lips. "There's a pretty little slut. Such a good girl. You want to suck on my cock, don't you, pretty girl?"

Stella's mouth opens wide and her tongue falls out in wanton desperation. Ronan glides his cock slowly inside, and her lips close around his girth. "You want to please us, don't you, Rabbit?"

Ronan, ever the smooth talker, manipulates her into thinking this is all her idea. I've seen him work his game on people, playing the role of the charming, handsome one who, of the three of us, looks fantastic on paper. He pulls out chairs, pays compliments, and has an easy way about him that people gravitate toward. He's the one we send in when we need a diplomat. Axel is the one we send in when we need to break heads, and I'm the one who goes in when we need to draw blood. If you see the three of us together, it's because we're bringing death. Which is precisely what we're doing here with Stella—killing the girl she thinks she is so the girl meant for us can be reborn.

Ronan pulls his cock out of her mouth with a pop. "Get on your hands and knees, Sweet Girl."

To my utter shock, Stella does what he asks without putting up a fight. She looks so hot in that position, her massive tits dangling, her large heart-shaped ass in view, sporting black cotton panties.

Axel bends down. His nostrils flare, and his eyes are consumed with unrestricted passion. He looks like an animal. He tears her panties straight off her large, sexy ass. "You've got the fuckin' hottest ass I've ever seen, Kitten."

Axel raises his hand above his head and lowers it to Stella's ass. It makes a loud smacking sound, causing her to scream and my cock twitch. But what fascinates me is she doesn't move her ass away. Instead, she pushes back.

Axel doesn't waste a moment; he slaps her again and again and again. "I love my handprint on your skin, Kitten. I want to mark you everywhere."

Before Stella can say anything, Axel shoves his cock deep in her pussy. "So tight, Kitten. So fuckin' tight. I always knew you'd be nice and wet for your big brother. You need to get in on this, Kian. You don't know what you're missing. Kitten here is a pretty whore, aren't you, Kitten?"

Axel pulls her back flush to him and slaps her tits, turning them the perfect shade of red. A surge of envy rips through me because I'm the one who wants to mark her skin, to show her the genuine pleasure wrapped in pain she'll receive at my hands.

My hands are on auto-pilot as I remove my thick leather belt from the loops of my pants and wrap it around my hand. Ronan is holding his dick, and as much as he doesn't get his kicks from threatening girls, he secretly likes to watch degradation and pain. He's a deranged fucker like the rest of us. He's just better at hiding it.

Stella's eyes widen as she watches me approach. Traces of fear linger in her eyes. She realizes I'm a monster. No point in hiding anything from her. She can see right through it. She isn't safe with me because what I crave is dark and twisted, completely depraved and violent. "These pretty pink tits need a little more blush."

I don't wait for her to register the belt before I bring it down on her massive tits. Her head falls back, and a shrill scream escapes her lips. "I'm not a complete monster, Stella. Stop looking at me like that!" I yell as I hit her again. This time her scream is not as shrill. Defiance, once again. I'll break her.

Axel glares at me—a warning shot. He might treat her like a whore, but he'll take my head off if I go too far with her. Always gotta toe Daddy's line, huh, your highness?

"Say "red" if you can't take it, Stella, and I'll make him stop," Axel says through gritted teeth.

The forest echoes with the smack of leather

on skin, over and over, but not once does Stella say "red."

I shove my face in front of hers, locking her dark brown eyes with my forest green gaze. "Say it, Stella. Say 'red.'"

She doesn't back down, not even the tiniest flinch. "No."

I raise my arm, belt in hand, ready to hit her again. "Say 'red,' Stella. Say it."

"No. Give me more."

I belt her again, and again, and again. My hand is becoming numb from the constriction of the belt, but Stella takes it all, shoulders pulled back, tits shoved directly in my face. "You're gonna look so pretty wearing all the marks I'm going to give your body."

9

STELLA

Ronan's tongue is quick-witted and talented. The way he moves the tip around my clit sends my entire body into overdrive. I understand why he's doing it, to help with the sting of the belt, but combined with the strikes Kian is giving me, it sets my entire body on fire. This isn't simply sex. It's a complete out-of-body experience.

The more I deny Kian, the harder he strikes. We've started a game, the two of us. It's a struggle for dominance, him desperate to hold on to it and me desperate to take it. I've lived my whole life in chaos, not sure what's going to happen, but for the first time, with these three men, my brain isn't moving in circles and working all the angles.

Ronan laps at my folds and places an uncharacteristically gentle kiss on my clit. It's almost loving in a fucked-up way. He rises and holds his dick, offering it to me. "Open up, Rabbit."

He moves into my mouth, his technique far gentler than Axel's. He isn't interested in showing dominance. It's as if he knows he's in control, a puppet master. Unlike Axel and Kian, Ronan isn't frantic in his command; he's precise and reassuring.

Axel degrades me, Kian punishes me, and Ronan encourages me. Different techniques, all meant to get the same result—my total submission.

"That's it. Suck my cock like a good girl," Ronan coos.

I swipe my tongue around his shaft, a sense of pride flooding me every time he groans.

"Shit," Axel grunts. "Her tight little cunt clenches every time you call her a good girl.

She's like a bitch in heat, desperate to be told she's worth something."

Axel strokes his fingertip over my clit as his huge dick thrusts furiously inside me. "You like being a good slut for Ronan, don't you, Kitten?" He isn't gentle, but his force is so addicting that my body succumbs to him even though my mind rages not to.

I mumble an incoherent "yes" on Ronan's dick as another sting lands on my skin from Kian's belt, this time along my back. He's merciless with his slashes that zigzag along my flesh.

"You're such a good girl, Rabbit." Ronan grabs my chin, forcing my gaze toward the bulge in Kian's pants. "It takes a lot to get Kian going. Look what you did to him, to all of us."

Pride blooms within me because I'm the one who has this effect on them.

"Get under her," Kian demands.

I'm unsure if he's talking to Ronan or Axel, but my question is soon answered when Axel moves under me and impales me onto him. He lifts my ass and opens my cheeks to expose my asshole to Kian's gaze.

"Kian, man, you can't go in her dry. This is going too far," Ronan warns.

Oh, God. The idea of him taking my ass virginity with no lube has my entire body shaking. I'll be subjected to unimaginable pain for God knows how long.

Cold liquid drips on my skin, trailing between my ass before three fingers glide along my crack and one inserts itself slowly into my asshole. Kian allows me to adjust before adding a second finger. Between his fingers sliding in and out of my asshole and Axel's thick cock in my pussy, I've never been so full.

"Who carries Vitamin E oil on them?" I hear Ronan ask.

"Someone who likes to fuck you up the ass," Kian says with a dark glint in his voice. "Lean over, Stella."

Kian covers my body with his and then presses the tip of his cock into my pussy, teasing me. My flesh strains as he lines his cock at my entrance and pushes the tip in slowly. It hurts at first. It's an intrusive sting, and I'm petrified. Neither man is small.

"Relax, Sweet Girl," Kian says as his hand soothes the welts he's left on my body. I let his voice wash over me and press my body into Axel's muscular arms.

"Head up, Rabbit," Ronan demands.

I raise my head to him, my mouth full of his thick cock. I'm in the middle of a forest, being fucked like an animal, and I love every fuckin' minute of it.

"They're right. You make a beautiful fuck hole. Look at you taking two cocks in your pussy and one in your mouth. You love this, don't you, Princess? You love being our little slut, don't you?"

They pull my head off Ronan's cock, holding my hair like a horse's reins. "He asked you a question, slut. Be a good girl and answer the man," Kian demands.

A wave of humiliation washes over me, not because of their demands but because of the truth in my words as I say, "I love being used like this. I'm nothing but a filthy slut. Use me like the whore I am."

My words seem to fuel Axel and Kian, and they bounce me back and forth between them and Ronan.

"That's a good slut. Bounce on our cocks, you greedy cock whore. Show us how badly you want our cum leaking out of your sexy cunt," Kian demands. "We're gonna stretch this cunt so good, baby. So good. Your pussy is going to weep to be stuffed by us and only us."

Kian pushes my head back on Ronan's cock, holding me still and fingering my ass while he and Axel push in and out of my pussy. I'm so full I may explode into the abyss. I can see my body becoming addicted to their touch, and the notion is spinning my entire world off its axis.

My body shakes, and an orgasm hits me so hard I think I'm going to shatter into a million pieces. I thought I'd had orgasms before, but they were tiny bursts of light. This one… this one is the fourth of July fireworks.

10

RONAN

You wouldn't think watching a woman get railed by three men would be a work of art, but that's exactly how Stella looks. I realize it sounds fucked up.

Hearing her whimpers over her gagging on my cock is so fuckin' hot. Mascara-ridden tears trail from her dark eyes down her round, soft face. Every time my best friends' hit her cunt and ass, she moans on my cock, sending vibrations along my spine. This girl is everything.

"We're going to fill you with cum, pretty girl," I rasp.

Her eyes shot up at my words, making my heart constrict. My balls tighten, and her eyes widen as I bust a nut deep in her throat. She tries to pull back, but I shove her down, holding her in place by the back of her head. There's no way she's wasting a drop. It's all for her. My pretty girl. "Drink it all down, Rabbit. You want to make me happy, don't you?"

Her head nods against my stomach as she mumbles on my cock. As much as coming down her hot throat is amazing, what I really want is to clean up her sweet pussy.

Neither Axel nor Kian are gentle as they fuck her with no mercy. Both are in her pussy, while Kian has three fingers deep in her ass. I'm relieved his cock isn't in there cause being fucked up the ass by Kian is no joke. I'm well aware of the shit he likes to pull, and if Stella isn't used to it, my girl will be sore. But as much as I worry about what they could do to her, I also know it will get me hard as fuck. Stella getting used by others is as hot as using her myself.

Kian pulls out. I'm not sure why because I

know he didn't come. He walks over to Stella and holds his cock to her face. "Clean off your dirty cunt, like a good whore." Stella moves to release my cock, but Kian stops her. "Tut, tut, slut. You can take us both in your mouth. You're so fuckin' chatty this might teach you a lesson about talking back."

Kian hooks his index finger along the side of Stella's mouth, pulling her cheek with my cock still lodged in her mouth. He grabs his cock and pushes it, rubbing it up against mine. He smears his blood-stained cock on her face, streaking her skin red. Hooking his index and middle finger on Stella's lips, he stretches her mouth to accommodate him as he glides his cock against mine. "Show us what a cock loving whore you are."

I slide my fingers along her soft skin, caressing her cheek. "It's okay." I'm a sick fuck cause she looks depraved, and I love it. Her mouth is too small to hold us, but Kian and I both push in, making her take it all. "You like this, don't you, Rabbit?"

Stella's muffled voice vibrates against our cocks, and Kian grunts. His hand wraps around her throat. "You want another load in your mouth, don't you, Sweet Girl? Well, it looks like today is your lucky day."

Kian stiffens, and cum shoots out of his cock into Stella's mouth. She can't hold with both our dicks lodged in her. White jizz seeps from the corners of her mouth, dribbling down her chin and landing on the hem of Kian's pants. His dick slides against mine as he pulls out of her and glares at the cum above the hem of his pants. Bending, he picks up the leather belt. "Looks like you've made a mess. Better clean it up if you don't want to get punished."

Rage flashes in Stella's chocolate eyes. She pushes off my cock, opens her mouth, and spits the cum into Kian's face. "Go fuck yourself."

Kian laughs. "I'd rather fuck you, Sweet Girl. Oh, wait. I already have." He smirks at her as he viciously yanks her hair and bends level with her face. His other hand moves along his face, cleaning the cum and spit before pushing his fingers violently to her lips. Stella fights the intrusion, her lips in a straight line, but Kian doesn't care. "Open your mouth, or I swear to God I'll belt your pussy so hard you'll wish you were dead." He pushes until it forces her lips to part, and he places all his fingers in her mouth, moving his cum back into her throat. "Now, isn't that better, Sweet Girl? So pretty," he says as he wipes her saliva into her face.

Kian is the most damaged out of the three of us. He never talks about why he's so fucked up, but his random screams in the middle of the night tell us how much trauma he holds inside his mind. It's most likely why he doesn't sleep and paints at all hours of the night. Like a mad man consumed with passion and running from demons.

"You okay, Rabbit?" I ask.

She nods.

"You're doing so well. I'm very proud of you."

Axel pulls Stella down to him. "Pour it into my mouth, Kitten."

Axel opens his mouth, and the flow of cum and spit from Stella's mouth pours into his.

"Fuckin' delicious." He guides her mouth down to his, and they swap the cum back and forth between them.

Watching my best friend and Stella snowball is so fuckin' hot my cock stirs again. Axel bounces Stella on his cock, and her head falls back as her tits jiggle, her round, smooth stomach leaning on Axel's rock-hard abs.

Kian grabs her nipples while Axel rubs her clit, and Stella and Axel come in unison through the pleasure and pain. The sight is perfect. Absolutely perfect.

I stroke her cheek before moving to where she's joined with Axel. I place my head between his legs and under her sweet cunt. He pulls out of her, his cum leaking from her sweet pussy. "Sit on my face, Stella."

"I'm not sitting on your face. I'll suffocate you," she protests.

"Sit on my face, or I'll let Kian belt your sweet cunt. Your choice, Stella. Another orgasm or a sore clit."

11

STELLA

OH, MY FUCKIN' GOD. Having someone eat you out after an orgasm is the most incredible sensation in the world. I might walk away from this in shame, but at this moment, I'm experiencing euphoria. I'm convinced Ronan is the devil himself with a tongue like this. His mother should have named him Lucifer.

Kian's fingers are still firmly on my nipples as he tugs, and Ronan's tongue laps at my pussy. I never desired to be with multiple men at once, but now I've experienced it, I'm not sure I can ever go back to one man again.

"This is going to make monogamous relationships hard from now on," I gasp.

"What makes you think we share, Kitten?" Axel demands.

I grind my pussy into Ronan's mouth, intensifying the desire building inside me. "I meant after today."

Kian laughs. "You're ours, Sweet Girl. There won't be other guys."

My orgasm takes over, and my body ignites as I sit firmly on Ronan's tongue. "Fuck you, Kian. You don't own me."

"You're ours now. We claimed you. Game over."

I'm trapped between ecstasy and hatred. As much as I want to deny them, Kian's words hold the truth. "I fucked you!" I scream. "Sex means shit."

Kian abandons my nipples to grip my jaw firmly. "You're never escaping me. If you try to fuck anyone other than the three of us, I'll kill the fucker. No one touches you ever again but us. It's not that bad, Kitten. You came what, three times? Maybe four?"

I want to tell him to take a hike. Lie and say his dick isn't special, none of theirs are, but I shut my mouth. Because the dark glint in his green eyes tells me he wouldn't bluff about taking someone's life if they so much as looked at me. I know without a doubt Kian is a cold-blooded killer. They all are.

Kian rubs his thumb against my bottom lip. "You're ours now, Stella. You better get used to it."

"Maybe for the summer, but you won't be around once I get a job and move out."

"Sweet Girl, we've been around since your senior year of high school. Ever wonder what happened to poor little Kevin Miller?"

My mind freezes. I stop moving against Ronan, but it doesn't matter because his firm hands grip my thighs, and he takes over.

Kevin Miller was a rapist. A piece of shit who raped three girls in high school. He never tried to rape me because I was the idiot who dated him willingly and gave it up without a fight. Two weeks after we had sex, he disappeared. A body never to be found. We assumed he'd left town, but it was Kian, Axel, or Ronan. Or all of them. "You killed Kevin?"

"Sure fuckin' did. We warned the fucker to leave you alone. He fucked you instead. No one fucks ours."

"Is this why every guy I've ever been with ends up disappearing or dumping me?"

Kian smirks. "We didn't fuck with all of them. One of them broke up with you. I broke his legs for dumping you. I wanted to kill him, but Rowan told me that was taking it too far."

"Why would you break his legs?" I demand. "He did exactly what you wanted?"

The corners of Kian's mouth turn up. The man is good-looking when he's all grouchy, but when he smiles, he is the most beautiful thing I've ever seen. "He made you cry. No one makes you cry."

"That's ludicrous. You've spent a good chunk of time here in the forest making me cry. You going to break your own legs now?"

Kian strokes his open hand against my cheek. I'm not sure if it's a loving touch or if he's rubbing the mascara and blood into new patterns. "Sweet Girl, the way we make you cry excites you. How that fucker made you cry broke your heart. "

I'm fucked in the head because that's the

most romantic thing I've ever heard. Or perhaps my pussy is in control because my brain has sure left the building.

Axel grips my waist and lifts me to my feet. "You did well, Kitten. I'm proud of you. Few people can handle all three of us like you did."

My heart constricts at his words. How many times have they done this? With how many women? I lower my eyes and brush my dress down, not wanting them to see me. I'm that invisible girl again, trying to hide from the rich, popular boys.

I shove my breasts back in my dress, smooth out my hair and turn from them. I'm about to run back to the house when Kian grabs my arm. "Where are you going, Kitten?"

"You had your fun. I'm going back to the house to pack my bags and return to campus."

"The fuck you are!" Ronan shouts.

But Ronan's outburst shocks me. He's been so calm and collected. I expected Kian to be the one to lose it. Part of me wants to laugh because his cheeks are covered in my blood. They kind of look like wings. Now I understand where the term redwings came from.

Ronan lunges for me, wraps his arms around

my waist, and pulls me to him. During the time we've been in the forest. Ronan has kept me centered. I expect Axel and Kian to use me how they want and not care about what I need, but for Ronan to be on board with that shakes me to my very core.

Ronan made sure I was comfortable, so having his powerful arms wrapped around my waist while he behaves like a madman is shocking.

I turn my head, and he looks away. The coward can't meet my eyes. I don't know why but Ronan behaving like the other two hurts my heart in ways I didn't think possible. I thought he'd keep me safe, but none of them will. I'm nothing but their toy.

Ronan casts his eyes to the ground, unable to meet mine, and whispers, "I'm sorry."

"Let go of me, Ronan," I demand.

"What are you not getting, Kitten," Axel asks.

His back is turned to me as he moves to the same tree Kian was leaning against when all this began. I watch in fascination as he reaches up between the branches and pulls down a camcorder. The blood drains from my face, and my heart drops to my stomach. He doesn't have to show me what's on the camcorder for me to know it's damning.

They've recorded everything. They have me in compromising positions. These men will use any means to get what they want. And they want me.

Axel turns to me. "I don't have to show you what's on here, do I, Kitten?"

"No," I whisper as a tear rolls down my cheek.

12

Ronan

I've never given a fuck what anyone thought of me. But seeing the hatred and anger in Stella's eyes makes me understand how it feels to have someone you care deeply about see you as nothing but trash. "You don't believe me, but I am sorry."

Stella whips around in my arms, fueled by adrenaline. Her eyes burn with fire, and her fists shake at her sides. My cock surges in my pants, and I want to bend her over and take her again to make sure she knows too much attitude is not a good idea unless she wants a sore fucking pussy. But I know I don't want to be like that with her. I want to show her how gentle I can be, how good it can be with the three of us.

"You're not fucking sorry, Ronan. Being sorry means you wouldn't do this, that you'd stop them. You're not sorry. You're a piece of shit." She whips around, glaring at Kian and Axel. "You're all trash."

I grab her underwear off the ground, hoping the tattered piece of cloth and my white handkerchief will make it better. "Here." I hand them to her. "You might be more comfortable if you use this. I'm sorry I don't have a tampon. I'll make sure you're as comfortable as possible tonight when you're in my room."

She whips them out of my hands but doesn't have time to put them on or use them. "I'm not fuckin' sleeping with you tonight."

Axel laughs and grabs her arm. "You gotta sleep with one of us. That's what we want. You're with us, either all together, one-on-one, or two on one. You can have one night for yourself, but you belong to us this summer. At the end of the summer, we'll give you the tape, and if you don't want to be with us, we'll let you go."

"Fine. I pick Kian," she says before heading back to the house, leaving us with a view of her sexy ass.

She fucking chose *Kian?* The motherfucker who belted her? Rage blooms in me, bursting in rays of light like a fucking atomic bomb. I lunge at her, grab her arm, and turn around to face me. "You fucking chose Kian?"

"Kian isn't a liar. I know exactly what I'm getting with him. A fucking psycho." She turns to Kian and offers her hand. "Guess being a prick will pay off for you tonight. Let's go!"

"Wait, you're picking him over me?" Axel demands.

Stella turns around, her long dark hair whipping in the wind. Her eyes smolder as she storms toward Axel and jabs him in the chest with her pointer finger. "Fuck you, Axel. You're the reason I'm in this mess."

Axel grins. "Wrong, Kitten. You're in this situation cause you had a little peep show at our expense."

13

STELLA

"What are you doing?" I ask, ripping the overnight bag out of Kian's grasp.

He rolls up the sleeves of his dress shirt as if preparing for a fight. "Packing."

"I don't know why you're packing me for now. Get the hell out of my room."

His moss-green eyes shroud with mischief, and he smirks at me. He grips my chin and growls a low visceral sound. "You already forgot our deal, Sweet Girl?"

"*Your* deal. I had no choice in the agreement."

Kian gazes at me. His intense stare takes in every inch of my body as if he's trying to process every part of who I am. I don't like it; I'm naked and not in the way I was in the forest. It's like he's seeing right to my heart and soul and exposing every dirty part of me. He's taking away my power and shifting it to him because with one look, he's done what they couldn't in the forest. Kian is the one I need to watch out for cause his cruelty isn't expressed with a belt or his hands. It's embedded in his mind.

"Do you want out?" he demands.

"Does it matter what I want?"

Kian takes a moment. His fingers move in the tips of my hair before he tucks a strand behind my ear. "Yes. If you tell me you want an out, I'll make sure you get it." He leans in, his deep voice caressing the shell of my ear. "It matters. As much as you want to think we don't give a fuck, the truth is we did all this cause we care too damn much."

"People who care don't coerce you."

"They do when it's the best thing for you."

"How is being your sex slave best for me?'

Kian chuckles. "You're avoiding the question."

"What question?'

"Do you want out?"

Kian's question is a ton of lead pushing against my heart. It's not a fair question. No matter how I answer, I lose. I could tell him I want out and never have to deal with them again. But it would be a lie because I've never been as wanted until these three men. They bring out something in me I've denied my entire life, and now it's released, I'm not sure I can go back to locking it up and ignoring it.

Kian takes a step forward, pushing me back. He smiles and does it again until my back hits the wall. "I'm waiting for an answer, Sweet Girl." He presses his nose to my neck and inhales. The act is so erotic, as if he's scenting me like an animal. "Do you want out?" he growls.

I want to say no, to show him I'm in charge here, to prove I hate him, hate all of them, but my lips can't formulate the lie my spite wants to tell. "No."

"Then pack up, buttercup, cause you're coming home with us."

"Home? Don't you all live here, in the manor?"

Kian shakes his head. "We have a penthouse on the North Side."

"The North Side of Chicago? Damn, y'all must have God money. Crime must pay well."

Kian shrugs as his fingers roam the spaghetti straps of my dress. "We do alright." He pulls me to him and slaps my ass. "Now, get packing."

— —

"That was amazing," I say to Kian as we pull into his parking spot, and he helps me off the back of his motorcycle. "The freedom on that bike."

"We can get you one."

"You'd let me drive a motorcycle?"

"Yes, why wouldn't I? You just need to get your license."

Axel's Porsche arrives, followed by Ronan's Lamborghini. I stare down at my target dress and dirt-covered knees and shame washes over me. I've never cared about money or material things, but the contrast of wealth between them and me is glaring.

"I don't like you riding the bike," Axel says.

I glower at him. "I don't give a fuck what you like."

Axel growls as he barrels toward me, grabbing my throat with force. "You will, Kitten. You'll be begging for my dick to do all kinds of things to your cunt. I promise you."

"Gonna be hard since I'm with Kian tonight," I snap before my foot connects directly with his balls.

He lets go of my neck and grabs them as he bends over on the ground.

Kian and Ronan wince and burst out laughing.

"I'll get you for that, Kitten," Axel wheezes.

"You'll have to catch me first!" I yell before running down the parking lot. I don't get too far before Axel grabs me around the waist and lifts me off the ground.

"Kitten, if you want my dick to stop being hard for you, you've gotta stop runnin' from me. You're turning me on with all this chasing."

"Fuck you!" I yell.

"That's the spirit, Kitten."

The audacity of this man. To think the entire world revolves around him. "How are you gonna manage that, Axel? Are you a rapist now?"

"Nah, I'll never rape you. I'd fuckin' shove a broken beer bottle up a guys ass if he ever tried to force himself on a woman. But you'll never say no to me, Stella. I bet if I touched my pussy, it'd be drenched."

"It's not your pussy."

Axel laughs. "Sorry, our pussy."

"MINE! IT'S MINE!" I screech.

"You keep telling yourself that, Kitten. But we both know we excite you, and the things we say and do to you make that cunt so wet you lose your damn mind."

I fucking hate him because he's telling the truth.

"Enough," Kian says, his hand on Axel's shoulder. "Give her a minute."

"That's rich, you telling me to calm down," Axel says, his voice low and lethal.

"Get your hands off her, Axel," Ronan demands. His voice is bitter, more lethal than I've heard before. "She needs to relax. We worked her hard today. She's not a fuckin' blow-up doll."

Axel's blue eyes blaze before he lets go of

me and walks away.

Kian's fingers twist in mine, holding my hand tight as if he's afraid I might disappear. "Let's go get you cleaned up."

Kian's room is nothing like I would expect. The walls are painted in vibrant colors that depict such passion it takes my breath away.

Kian, the man who normally sports a scowl and grunts when speaking, seems to value beauty. I don't know what I expected, but it wasn't this. "Who painted these murals?"

Kian drops my overnight bag beside his bed and looks up at me. "I did."

"You paint?"

"Paint, draw, sculpt."

I trail my fingers along the girl with the dark hair etched in the mural. My eyes wander, and I notice the same girl on every wall. "Who's the girl?"

He gazes at me, tilting his head slightly to the side with a perplexed look as if I'm asking an idiotic question. "You."

14

KIAN

I should have lied when she asked who the girl in the murals was cause now she has a faraway look in her eyes as she regards my work. I don't want her thinking I'm some prince and she's Snow White, singing and dancing with the birds and other animals in the forest. If this is a fairytale, I'm Rumpelstiltskin or The Wolf. She's not safe with me because *I'm* not safe with me. There's a darkness lurking inside me, a twisted, all-consuming desire. It's the part of me she should be afraid of because it's the strongest when she's around.

"You paint?"

"I have since high school. I used to sketch before that."

"How long have you been painting me?"

I'm relieved she doesn't ask why she's on every painting. I answer truthfully. "Since the first time I saw you. Your senior year. You were in the locker room, your eyes wide as you watched. You looked scared, but you didn't run or hide. You watched us with a sense of awe, which started my fascination with you."

"More like an obsession," she whispers.

"Is that so bad? Having three grown men obsessed with you?"

Confusion flickers on her stunning face as she looks at me. Her eyes flash to the easel set up by the large glass window. "Will you show me what you're working on?"

"Let's get you cleaned up before we do anything else?" I reach out for her hand, and to my surprise, she takes it with no struggle.

She sits on the leather bench in the washroom's corner. I've got no idea why it's there.

Rich women like random shit, and the interior decorator Axel hired has eccentric tastes.

I run the water in the giant bathtub. "'You want bubbles?"

"No, I'm not sure I can relax enough here to enjoy it."

I don't like that I make her tense. She shouldn't be afraid of me, of us. In reality, she's the only person who shouldn't be. "Get in the tub, Sweet Girl."

She doesn't move. "Can you turn around?"

"No. You're fuckin' beautiful, and I enjoy looking at beautiful things."

"I'm far from beautiful."

"Stella, every inch of you is perfect. From your big tits to your sexy heart-shaped ass. I dream about your thick thighs wrapped around my neck while you ride my mouth to orgasm."

I pull her to the large floor-length mirror and slip the straps of her dress off her shoulders, so it slides down her body and pools at her feet. "Open your eyes, Stella. Look at yourself."

I place kisses along her shoulder before moving down her body, gently capturing her nipple in my mouth and tugging. I trail down her body and kiss the beautiful stretch marks adorning her stomach like abstract art.

I fall to my knees. My fingertips grip her panties, and I drag them down. She gazes at me before swiftly looking away. "Keep your eyes on the mirror, Sweet Girl. I want you to see what I see. Every single inch of you is perfect. Every part of you gets me rock hard. You're beautiful, Stella. A fucking work of art."

She intakes a shaky breath as I kiss her pussy, moving down her legs until I reach her feet and place a kiss on each foot. "Now be a good girl and get into the tub."

She sighs as I massage the shampoo into her scalp. "That feels so good."

I chuckle. "Well, I want you to relax."

I dip my hand under the faucet, checking the water temperature before rinsing the excess shampoo from her dark hair.

"Where did you learn to wash hair?"

I give her locks a playful tug. "I know I'm

an artist, but we do bathe. That dirty artist thing is an atrocious stereotype."

"No, don't be silly. I mean, how can you wash hair with such care and tenderness? Usually, this is the service one finds at a salon. I would never have expected a man like you to wash hair like this. You got a secret identity you're not telling me about?"

"I used to wash my mother's hair." I've no idea why I told her the truth. My mother is a topic I don't discuss with anyone. Besides Axel and Ronan, no one knows where I came from, so I don't know why I'm telling her things. I've buried the memories so deep I've forgotten them myself.

"Was she sick?" Stella asks, her voice shaking. I don't like that she's scared to ask me hard questions.

"Yes. I don't talk about her much. My dad left when I was ten. He married a woman twenty years younger and started a new family in California. My mom never got over it. She started drinking, and that led to drugs. I spent my childhood caring for a heroin addict who could barely get out of bed, let alone wash her hair." I pour the conditioner over her head and rub my fingers through her hair.

"Conditioner? What did I do to deserve this five-star treatment?"

I'm relieved she doesn't press about my mother. "You deserve way more than this, Stella."

"Can I see you paint?"

I freeze. When I paint, I'm manic. It's like darkness takes over my body. The paintings don't come out dark, not all the time, but the part of me that creates art isn't light. I've let no one view my paintings or sketches, but I've never had someone I care about ask to see them.

I rinse the conditioner from her hair, hoping she'll relax and forget all about me and the art. Maybe she's too tired, and once I tuck her into bed, she'll pass out, and that will be the end of the conversation.

I remain silent as I lift her out of the tub. Water sloshes on the ground, soaking my shirt and pants. I grab the fluffy white towel from the towel rack and wrap it around her. "Sit," I say, placing her on the bench and grabbing a brush.

She sighs and lets me brush her hair, getting all the tangles out. "You've got a lot of welts from the belt." I gently trace my fingers along one of the lash marks. "Does it hurt?"

"A little."

"Why didn't you say 'red'?"

She shrugs. "In the forest, it was about proving something. I didn't want to be scared. I needed to prove I was in control."

"You don't need to prove you're in control, Sweet Girl. You are." I chuck my shirt and stand beside her, my chest bare. I whip off my belt and hand it to her.

"What do you want me to do with that? Strangle you?"

"No," I laugh. "I want you to whip me. Payback and all."

"I don't want to. Truth is, I liked all of it."

"What do you want, then?"

"I want to watch you paint."

15

STELLA

I'm taken aback by how gentle Kian is. He's a wild animal in the forest, but the remorse in his eyes while he gazes at the marks from the lashes he gave me cracks a piece of my heart.

I rub my thighs together as I take in his sculpted chest and how his pants ride low on his hips, exposing the perfect V.

He tugs at my hand, forcing me off the bench, and walks me to a giant glass window.

I'm not worried about anyone seeing my flesh because the penthouse is so high, like a tower overlooking the Chicago skyline. "What are you doing?"

He dips his head in the crook of my neck. "You want me to paint, don't you, Stella?"

My throat catches, but I manage a raspy, "Yes."

He slips his robe from my shoulders, exposing my flesh to his predatory eyes. "Then I'm gonna need some inspiration." He pushes me back until my legs hit the back of the wing-back chair next to his easel. "Have a seat, beautiful, and spread your legs for me. Show me my pussy."

My body ignites under his intense stare. Something animalistic and dominant in his eyes hits my clit, making my center pool with moisture. "Don't close your legs. I might need a snack."

He turns and unveils a half-finished painting. It's beautiful. A forest with two guys kissing. A girl is tied to a tree, and another man is eating her out. It's erotic and dirty and does all kinds of things to my body because it forces me to remember everything they made me experience today.

Kian paints like the wind. It's graceful and dangerous. His hands swipe along the canvas with no apparent method to his madness, but as soon as he's done, pretty leaves appear on the trees or debris on the forest floor. It's magic. I've never seen anything as mesmerizing as watching Kian paint.

I'm so lost regarding this man make beautiful art that I miss his frustrated sigh. He goes from dancing with his hands to throwing his brush against the wall and his hands fisted by his side.

"What's wrong?"

"None of these reds are right," he spits in frustration.

"Can you blend them?"

"No, I've tried. It's not right."

My eyes flash to Kian's hand, moving across various pallet knives before it stops on a silver, pen-shaped Exacto knife. He grips the metal in his hand before turning to me. My heart pounds violently in my chest, not out of fear but excitement.

"Hold still, Stella." His voice is dark and erotic.

I keep my position, not budging as he walks toward me and bends down. His eyes are on my pussy as one of his hands roams up my thigh, and the other holds the Exacto knife.

He stops right at the juncture where my pussy meets my thigh. "Be a good girl and hold still."

His tongue laps at my folds as the sharp point of the Exacto knife slices my skin. The sting of the blade and the blissful pleasure of his tongue on my clit are so euphoric I think I'm having some sort of out-of-body experience. Kian moves his mouth from my pussy and licks the cut he made.

He rises, returns a moment later with a fine art brush, and dips it into my blood. "This. This is the shade of red I was looking for." Kian paints with my blood as if it's the most normal thing on the planet.

When he finishes, he places the brush down and gazes at me. His eyes hold a softness, a shocking tenderness from a man like Kian. "This is who I am, Stella. I'm not someone who will bring you roses or make you candlelight dinners. That's why we're okay with sharing you. Ronan will provide you with those things. Axel will push you, and I will set you on fire. We've been looking for someone to complete us. That's you. But I promise no one will hold you against your will. The choice has to be yours. You have to want to be ours. We're not whole, not good enough for you on our own, but the three of us together will make you happy. We'll make you the center of our fucked-up world."

My heart constricts at his words, and I nod, not sure I know what else to say.

Kian walks over and lifts me off the chair before carrying me to the bed. He spreads my legs, moves his head to my pussy, and starts eating me out. His tongue works furiously but carefully as he flicks my clit and sucks it between his teeth. He inserts nothing in me, just glides his tongue along my flesh, making my entire body shiver in desperate need.

"Be a good girl and hold still. Daddy is hungry. You taste so good, Sweet Girl. I want you to be the last thing on my tongue every night before I go to bed and the first thing every morning when I wake up."

My hands tangle in his sheets, my hips buck up, and I come. Kian kisses my pussy before he lifts me and tucks me under the covers. "Sweet dreams for my Sweet Girl."

16

Axel

Two. A.M.

Another night where I can't sleep. It's been two weeks, and Stella hasn't spoken to Ronan or me. She's been sleeping with Kian every night as if she belongs to him. She doesn't, and I'm tired of waiting.

Ronan keeps saying we need to give her time, but fuck that. Two weeks is plenty of time. There's no way in fuckin' hell I'm gonna give up and let Kian have her. I hear her at night fucking him, refusing to let us in. Ronan and I have been fuckin each other pretending it's her cunt we're lost in, like pathetic love sick puppies.

I toss the sheets off me and walk down the hall to the kitchen, stopping dead in my tracks. There she is, sitting quietly, sipping from a mug.

The moonlight hits her face, making her appear transcendent, like a fucking angel sent from heaven. She's this perfect, pure thing lusted after by demons who want to violate and defile her.

I could stare at her for the rest of my life and be content. She's that miraculous. It should be a sin to be as attractive as her, to walk around in society among common folk.

I want to hide her from all prying eyes yet show her off like the prized diamond she is. No other woman on this planet could hold a candle to her, and here she sits in the dark, not realizing the power she wields with her undeniable beauty. No one else, man or woman, could hold a candle to her.

Sure, I love the guys. Both of them are parts of me, but Stella is my heart. She completes me. She completes all of us. She makes us a family. Now I need to convince her to stay.

I'm a piece of shit for bribing her. We all are, but she's the blood running through my veins, the last thing I see when I close my eyes at night, and the first person I think about when I wake up in the morning. I can't tell you why she's so important to me. She just is. Some things can't be explained, and my need for Stella is one of those things.

She takes another sip of her drink and licks her lips, causing my dick to twitch in my pants. She doesn't realize I'm there. Maybe that's one blessing of being a killer. You can watch your prey for days on end without them knowing you're there, and when they notice you, it's too late.

I walk up to her, keeping my steps light so she doesn't notice me. Right behind her, I stop. I'm so close I can smell the shampoo in her raven hair. My fingers twitch with the need to grab those ebony locks and yank her head back. But right now, it's time to show her everything I want to do to her.

I bend down, placing my mouth on her ear. "Miss me, Kitten?"

She jumps, and the mug flies from her hand, crashing to the ground. It smashes and spills its contents onto the floor. "Axel."

"Yes, little sister, it's me."

She blanches my name for her, but she doesn't correct me. After her performance in the forest, I know what my kitten needs. She likes to pretend she's a good girl, but for me, she's always gonna be bad.

"Did that make your pussy wet?"

She tries to move away from me, but I tug back with the use of her hair and hold her still. "I asked you a question, little sister. Does your big brother make your sweet cunt wet?"

She doesn't answer me, and I pull her hair until she's facing me.

"If you want me to stop, let me know."

"I don't want you to stop," she whimpers.

I wrap my other hand around her neck, and her pretty brown eyes widen. But it's not fear in her eyes. It's lust. My kitten likes this little game as much as I do. I move toward her, and she retreats until her back is against the floor-to-ceiling windows.

She's wearing Kian's robe and takes a deep breath as my fingers play with the knot holding it together. "Tell me what you want big brother to do to you, sis."

"Touch me down there," she whispers.

"Touch, you where? Use your big girl words."

She glares at me, her eyes flashing venom, but she says the words I want to hear. "Touch my pussy, please."

"Aren't you a dirty slut, begging for your big brother to touch your wet cunt?"

"Yes," she pants. "I'm a filthy slut."

Shock rocks through me at her words. I'm not expecting her to partake in the dirty talk, but goddamn, it's hot as fuck.

I squeeze her breasts, and she whimpers. "You make me hard as fuck. Driving me crazy for five fuckin' years. I should punish your cunt for all the years of torture. Show you how naughty you are by letting you walk around with a sore pussy." I pinch her nipple between my fingers.

Stella pushes her hips forward, her body begging me to provide her relief. As much as I want to tease her, the need to be buried deep inside her is greater.

I move my hand between her legs, rubbing

my knuckles on her bare cunt and feeling how drenched she is. "So wet for me, baby. Tell me you want your brother's cock in your pussy."

"I want your cock in my pussy," she repeats.

Not good enough. "No, little sister. I want you to call me your brother and beg for my cock like a good whore."

"Please, fuck me. I want my big brother's thick cock deep in my tight pussy. Show your little sister how much you want her sweet cunt."

"Thatta girl. Lock your leg around my waist."

Stella wraps her leg around me. I unbuckle my belt and unzip my pants, dropping them to the ground. I don't need any prep work. One look at her, and I'm hard as a rock. I grab her wrists in one hand and slam her arms above her head. I line my cock up with her entrance and go in with one rough thrust.

"Oh, god," Stella moans as she gazes down to where we're joined.

"You're taking your big brother's cock so well. You're a dirty girl, aren't you, little sis?" I pull out of her, and she sighs in protest. I flip her around and press her tits against the windowpane. "Stare out at the city, sister. Look at how open and exposed you are. Imagine someone out there watching you fuck your brother like a whore, whacking off their thick cocks thinking about your sweet cunt being railed by your brother."

17

STELLA

Axel's words are dirty and taboo, and they should turn every part of me off because they're sick and twisted. But they don't. The more he talks, the more I want him, and the more I crave him.

Axel's hands are rough. He grabs my side and squeezes, making me yelp. "What are you, sis?"

"A dirty girl," I whisper.

Axel pulls my hair, his cock pounding mercilessly into me. He grazes his teeth against my shoulders until he meets the delicate part of my neck. He kisses me there sweetly before he sinks his teeth in, cutting through the skin. The bite hurts, but the pain doesn't last long because Axel's finger is on my clit as he laps at the blood trickling from my neck.

"I want to mark every part of you. Sink my teeth into every inch of your flesh. I'm going to take you rough, Stella. It's going to hurt, but know this: I'll always protect you. I'll be the best big brother."

His hand moves back to my throat, his grip tighter than before. He's pressing so hard I think I might pass out or die.

He pulls my head to the side. "Open wide for big brother."

I barely have my mouth open before he spits into it. The act is so degrading but so hot.

"Swallow my spit, Kitten. Show big brother how well his little slut sister listens." I swallow, and Axel smiles. "Good girl."

"What's happening here?" a deep voice asks behind us. Ronan. "Is this a private party, or can anyone join?"

Axel slaps my face with his free hand while his fingers constrict my throat. "Want Ronan to join us, sis, or do you wanna keep big brother's cock all to yourself?"

He forces his fingers in my throat, gagging me as he continues to pound his enormous cock into me, moving faster and faster, in and out. I'm lost in the misty fog of pain and pleasure, making it hard to concentrate on his question. He restricts my vocal cords between his fingers in my mouth and his hand around my throat, making it hard for me to breathe. My arms are plastered to the window above my head as if conditioned to stay in place. He's a puppet master, and I'm his puppet. I'm in ecstasy because I like not having control.

Not thinking relieves the pressures that have been on me my entire life. I've always had to worry about myself, Mom, and school. All the things a child shouldn't be concerned with have weighed heavily on my shoulders.

"I want him," I gasp, trying to speak with my vocal chords restricted.

"Where do you want him, Kitten?" Axel moves his fingers toward my ass. "Do you want Ronan in your ass while your brother pounds your pussy, or do you want your big brother to take you from behind while you suck Ronan's big fat dick?"

"I want you to fuck me while Ronan fucks you."

"Is that what you want, Kitten? For your bother to be fucked up the ass while he fucks his sweet little sister's cunt?"

"Yes," I pant. "Ronan, fuck my big brother. Cum in his ass while he cums in my pussy."

I've never been a vocal person during sex. Not that I've had much, but I feel like I can let go with these three. They won't look down on me when I ask for what I want. They'll encourage it. They may be unorthodox and do things that would make them evil in the eyes of many, but when it comes to me, it's different. They treasure me. They value me, and most of all, they need me as much as I need them.

Ronan steps up to me, and our eyes lock. He presses his lips roughly to mine, but I crave the need behind them. One hand fists my hair while the other grips my jaw as his tongue probes my mouth, and our tongues dance in a battle of wills. The kiss is passion combusting in need, and I'm consumed by it.

Ronan grabs my hand from the glass

window and places it on his cock. "If you want me to fuck him, you better get on your knees and make me nice and hard, Rabbit."

Axel grabs my waist, lifting me away from the window, and bends me over. He's still pounding my pussy, my legs straight as I fold at the waist, my eyes level with Ronan's cock. "Be a good girl and suck Ronan's dick for your big brother. Show me what a wonderful cock sucker my little sister is."

Ronan drags the tip of his cock along my lips. My tongue slips out, and the salty taste of his pre-cum hits my senses. He grips my hair, and I open wide as he slips his thick cock into my mouth. I relax my throat, letting him push further in until he hits my gag reflex.

Ronan holds my face firmly as he pounds back and forth with his long cock. "You're doing such a good job, Princess. Get my dick nice and wet so I can fuck your brother for you. Do you get wet at the idea of my big dick fucking Axel?"

Ronan pushes further down my throat, fucking it like it's my pussy. He grabs my hair and pulls my head back so his cock falls out of my mouth. Drool flows from my lips, falling down my naked body and gliding down my breasts. I'm depraved and I don't care.

"What are you, Rabbit?" Ronan demands.

"A good little slut." I say the words not because they want to hear them but because I want to say them. Those words give me power. They give me control.

Ronan strokes his fingers through my hair. "You're such a good girl, Rabbit. You deserve a reward." He slides under me and starts licking my clit, wrapping his legs around my head and pulling me down between his legs.

"Suck his cock, little sister. Suck his cock nice and good while your brother fills your pussy with cum. I'm gonna fill you with so much cum, sister. I'm gonna fill that belly nice and full. You on the pill, Kitten, or am I gonna put a baby in you?"

Axel's words are filthy, encouraging me to swallow Ronan's cock in my mouth and go as deep as I can. I want Ronan to abuse my throat, to hit the back and make me gag, to use me as his personal toy. Every time I gag on his dick, I am thrown further into the depths of depravity.

Ronan's tongue is on my clit, and Axel's cock is hitting my G-Spot. Between the two of them, I see stars. I don't know how they can make my body feel this good, but they're magicians. They've captivated me. My body can't take it anymore. The burning need, the desire builds within me, and my body shakes as my fingers dig into Ronan's thighs. His blood is now under my skin. I want to say something, but I can't. Ronan's calves are on my head, holding me still. I can't do anything other than suck his cock and take Axel's rough pounding in my pussy.

I scream with my mouth wrapped around Ronan's dick as I come in waves on Axel's dick, and with a visceral grunt, he floods my pussy with his cum.

18

RONAN

She tastes perfect. If there's one perfect flavor in this world, it's Stella's pussy.

Axel grunts one last time as he pulls out of her, and his cum leaks from her cunt. I latch on to her pussy, sucking his cream into my mouth. I love eating cum, and the mixture of Axel's and Stella's cum is so fuckin' erotic I could blow my load from the flavor.

I hold the cum in my mouth, gently push Stella off my cock, and get up. Axel and I make eye contact, and I grab him by his neck, and he opens his mouth. I bring my mouth to his and spit his cum inside. When I pull away, a string of saliva-mixed cum connects us.

“Get over here, Kitten, “I demand. “Before I fuck your brother’s ass, I want you to get some of his hot cum in your mouth.”

Stella walks over to Axel and opens her mouth while I spread coconut oil along his ass cheeks. My fingers find his asshole, and I push in with coconut oil to get him nice and ready for my cock. Axel groans as he spits his cum into Stella’s mouth.

“Drink up your brother’s cum like a good girl,” I demand as she swallows, not wasting a single drop. “Go sit on a chair and spread your legs. Big brother is going to stare at your cunt while I fuck him deep in the ass.”

Stella does as she’s told. Her pussy glistens underneath the moonlight. Fuck, who knew a pussy could be so fuckin hot? I could spend my entire life staring at her pretty, pink cunt. My mouth waters at the idea of tasting her again, but she wants me to fuck Axel, and that’s what I’m going to do. That she’s touched us alone is a good sign. The girl can hold a grudge like no other. Two weeks since the incident in the forest, and she's shut us completely out until now. So I'm going to fuck Axel up the ass because I want her happy. I also like fuckin' Axel.

I push my fingers into Axel's hair and pull his head back. "He's so tight, Rabbit. You should see how his ass is swallowing my fingers. I've got two digits in his ass right now. Do you want me to put in another and make it three, or should I shove my cock deep inside him?"

"Put another finger in him," she ruthlessly demands.

I smile at her eagerness. Our girl is accepting her darker side and claiming her sexuality. She knows she's safe with us, and it's the biggest fuckin' turn-on.

"I want you to tell him how hot he looks bent over for you."

"You look good, Bro. You're making me so wet. Your little sister's pussy is dripping at the idea of her big brother getting fucked up the ass for her." Stella dips her finger into her cunt before sticking it out in front of us. "Wanna taste it, brother? Want my cum on your tongue while you get rammed up your tight ass by Ronan's thick dick?"

Holy shit, the mouth on her. My cock is throbbing as it drips pre-cum.

"Feed me that cream. Put it on your brother's tongue and let me savor that sweet cunt," Axel pants.

Axel shuffles his body forward, sticking out his tongue. Rabbit holds her fingers out of reach. I admire her. She's giving us a taste of our own medicine. Letting us know how strong she is.

I remove my fingers from Axel's ass and line up my cock. "Ready to watch me fuck your brother? Do you want me to stretch him nice and wide for you?"

Axel grunts as I push my cock in his ass. I allow him to adjust before I push in further. "Tell your sister how good my cock feels in your tight ass, Axel. Tell her how full you are and how much you love it."

"His dick is so good, little sister. You like your brother getting fucked by his best friend. Is your pussy wet watching this? You want me to lick your cunt, don't you? I am going to suck and bite that hot clit until you come, screaming my name. I want your cream to flood my mouth while Ronan's cum drips out of my ass."

"Bring the chair closer, Rabbit," I order.

She rushes behind the wing-back chair, shuffling it on the floor until it's directly in front of Axel. She sits seductively, placing one leg over each arm of the chair.

Axel's nose is directly in her cunt. He inhales so loudly that we both hear it. Axel's head buried deep in Stella's cunt is so fucking hot it almost drives me over the edge. "Is your brother doing a good job licking your sweet pussy?"

Stella's hands are in Axel's hair, holding him on her pussy. She bucks her hips, pushing into his face even more. "Yes, big brother, eat that pussy. Show me how much you want me, how much you need me. Make me come all over your face."

I maneuver my hand and grab Axel's cock. He's hard as steel again. I rub his dick with a coconut oil-covered hand. Tugging back-and-forth as I keep ramming his ass with my dick. He moans loudly, in complete bliss. Attention paid to his asshole, his cock, and his tongue deep in his sister's sweet pussy. I'm a little jealous of Axel right now. The best of two worlds.

19

AXEL

I'm going to fuckin' come again. Ronan is jerking me perfectly, moving his hand up and down in a quick motion while his cock hits me in all the right places. And fuck, Stella's cunt is so fuckin' juicy, so perfect. The girl gushes, and it's making me wild. I want her to drown me in her cum. I want to be buried in it.

"Where do you want my cum, Stella? In his ass, or do you want me to come on his face?"

"In his asshole. I want to watch it drip down

his legs. So fuckin' hot seeing you fuck like this. Finger me, Axel. Finger me and let me come to your face. Make it all nice and wet. I want Ronan to lick my cream off you. I want you two to share my juice."

Holy fuck. As soon as she says those words, my cock jerks in Ronan's hand. I'm on the brink of blowing my load.

"I'm going to come," Ronan grunts, and his jizz floods my asshole.

I put my fingers in Stella's pussy, twisting them and hitting her G spot as I suck her clit between my lips. She tugs my hair, pulling me down as she raises her hips off the chair and grinds her cunt into my face. She fucks my face as she screams her orgasm and floods my mouth with her sweet cum.

Cum slips out of my ass and glides down the back of my legs when Ronan pulls out of me.

Ronan keeps tugging on my cock until my cum spurts out in his hand and lands on the marble floor. He walks over to Stella, smirking as he wipes his cum-stained hands on her face. "Such a pretty girl. So pretty covered in your big brother's cum."

Stella swipes some cum from her lips and

offers it to me. I open my mouth and suck her finger as Ronan licks her cheek. "Fuckin' delicious."

"Seems like I missed all the fun," Kian says, standing by the island. "Stella, go shower, and then we all need to talk."

"Talking is so overrated. I'm a man of action," Ronan says, grabbing his cock.

"You should probably get cleaned up, too," Kian says, all humor gone from his voice.

20

STELLA

We sit at the kitchen island, mugs in hand. The guys nervously take sips of coffee as we all watch Ronan working at the stove.

"How come you can cook?"

It's odd that Ronan is such a phenomenal cook, growing up the way he did. He's cooked every meal since we've been here. He's not a decent chef, he's Michelin star excellent.

I melt as Ronan flashes his dimples. "I spent most of my life in hotels. My dad would be away on business, and my mom was always on set. I figured I'd be eating takeout for the rest of my life if I didn't learn how to cook."

I turn to Kian. "So, what do we need to talk about? How you kidnapped me, held me against my will, and coerced me into having sex with you?"

Kian glares at me. Something lurks behind his emerald-green eyes—there's always something lurking behind Kian's eyes. Out of the three guys, he's the one who has the greatest darkness and sadness in him. He told me a little about his past, but there's still so much I don't know.

Ronan seems to be the most well-adjusted. To the outside, there's nothing wrong with him. He's beautiful, rich, and has an energy that effortlessly attracts others. Ronan is very likable. No one would think this handsome, amiable guy is a ruthless killer.

Axel, the spoiled one of the three. I can't help the tingle between my legs when I remember how he was used by Ronan earlier. The taboo and depraved things he said or made me say to him were so hot. I'll never be able to go without it now. Axel is the one who woke me. He's the one who got me addicted to these three men. He's the ringleader. And the one at who all my anger is directed.

"We don't want you for the summer anymore," Kian says.

I should be happy, but my heart constricts, and pain almost makes me topple over.

I guess once they got what they wanted from me, it became easy to let me go. I never believed they cared about me. I was a plaything for them to use and abuse and throw in the trash like useless garbage.

It hurts. I knew their reputation. They go on one or two dates, and the woman is history. None of them had a girlfriend during or after high school. It was naïve of me to think I was the exception because I'm another rule.

I rise from my chair and look at the three of them as I fight back tears, willing them to stay put and not fall down my cheeks. "If that's what you all want, I'll pack up my bags and call an UBER. Have a pleasant life, guys."

I turn my back on them as one tear slowly escapes. They might as well have stabbed me in the heart. It would have hurt less than this raw, empty feeling. I take one step, and a strong hand grabs my wrist.

"Whoa, there, Kitten," Axel says. "Where do you think you're running off to?"

"I'm leaving like you asked. "

"You can't leave." Kian gets up so fast he kicks the stool behind him, and it lands with a thud on the floor. "You're not going anywhere."

"You're giving me whiplash!" I shout. "You all told me you want me to leave."

"No!" Kian shouts back. "We gave you the option to leave or stay based on your free will."

"So, what the fuck do you want from me?" I shout at all of them.

Ronan pushes past Kian and walks over to me. He grabs my face in his hands, his eyes searching mine. "We want you to stay. Stella. We want it to be your choice."

"That's funny," I spit. "Because I swear Kian told me I can't leave. So you're not giving me a choice."

Ronan rubs his thumb along my bottom lip. "Don't worry about Kian. We all want you. We need you. But if push comes to shove, we'll do what's best for your happiness. We want you to be happy, and if you honestly don't want to be with us, we'll keep each other in check and let you do what you wish."

My eyes cast down to the marble, and I focus on the white, gray, and black colors blending together. "I don't want to leave."

21

KIAN

I *don't want to leave.*

Those words lift ten tons of lead off my chest. The relief in my body is so heady I have to sit down.

"Thank fuck." Ronan says as he laces his fingers in hers and walks her back to the island.

She moves to sit down, but I grab her hips and pull her on top of me.

"What are you doing?" she squeals.

"You're gonna have breakfast on my lap,

Sweet Girl." I watch the blush on her face, and she pushes her long locks behind her ears. "Sweet Girl, this is nothin' to blush about, But I can give you something that'll make you turn red."

I lift her and place her on the island. Pushing her legs open, I tuck my hands under them. "Lift your hips for me."

I smile when she obeys without objection and lets me pull her panties down her long legs. I grab the plate of berries Ronan put on the table and bring it between us.

"What are you doing?" she asks, her eyes roaming my face for a tell.

"I'm having dessert before breakfast," I nod towards her pussy, "and I like cream with my berries."

I stare at her pussy. She's already wet with anticipation. I trail the tip of a strawberry around her clit. "I love how you're always wet and ready for us. It's like your pussy knows who it belongs to." I push the strawberry into her cunt and make sure it's covered in her sweet juice before putting it to my mouth and taking a bite. "Fuckin' delicious."

"I'd like some of that cream," Axel says as he pushes a raspberry in Stella's pussy and licks it before popping the berry in his mouth.

Stella's head falls back, her huge tits pushed out, and her legs spread wider of their own accord.

"Look at you, Sweet Girl. Spread out on the island like a dirty slut. Allowing your brother and his friends to feast on your cunt." I slap her pussy and she yelps, her hips bucking toward me as if begging for more. I smirk at her before waking over and removing a spatula from the canister by the stove.

"You need to taste how good this cream is, little sis," Axel says as he pushes a strawberry between her lips.

Stella's eyes close as she takes a bite with a look of orgasmic bliss plastered all over her pretty face.

As she's savoring the berry, I slap her pussy with the flat end of the spatula. "Such a dirty girl, Stella. Your legs opened like a wanton slut, letting us dip berries in that sweet cunt. You like being used, don't you, Stella?

"Yes," she pants.

"You like being our whore, don't you, Sweet Girl?"

"God, yes."

I spank her pussy again. "No one will make this sweet pussy as wet as us, isn't that right?"

"Yes, Jesus, please."

"You're ours." Spank. "Our whore." Spank. "Our slut." Spank. "Our love." Spank. "You're ours now and forever." Spank. "Only ours."

"Oh, my god. I'm coming!" Stella screams, bucking her hips in the air.

I spank her clit one more time. "Ours to make come."

I drop the spatula and bury my mouth on her pussy, licking her clit, wanting to drown in her scent and taste.

"Jesus!" Stella screams.

I chuckle into her pussy. "Not Jesus, baby. The only person who can make you come this hard is the devil himself."

"Shit, as much as I want this to continue, we need to get going," Axel says.

"What?" Stella asks. "Where are we going?"

"We have to meet some people for business," Axel responds.

Stella frowns. "Your illegal business?"

Ronan touches Stella's shoulder. "Stella, we are who we are. We aren't good men, and we never claimed to be. But we'll always be good to you. Now get that fine ass in gear. We want to show you off."

22

STELLA

Never in my life did I think I'd be sitting at a table in a dark corner of a restaurant with my mafia boyfriends and their business contacts.

Are they my boyfriends?

There are three other men there, all in pristine, over-priced suits, one of them in a creepy white mask. My body chills thinking about what he's hiding under there. Unlike the other two men, he's on alert, taking in our surroundings like he's in a dangerous war zone. A pretty woman with soft eyes in jeans and a t-shirt sits closer to one of the men. Like me, she doesn't seem like she belongs.

"Stella, this is Max Fedrovah and his brother Alexie. The one in the mask is Mikhail. Don't worry, he's safe, at least for us," Axel says, his arm resting on my lower back. "And this beauty here is Samira."

"Watch it," the one named Max growls, wrapping his arm around Samira possessively.

Axel smirks. "Would you like me to use stunning as an adjective to describe your wife instead?"

Samira places her hand on Max's chest, and instantly his expression goes from anger to pure adoration. "Max, I'm gonna take Stella to the bar while you all talk about whatever you need to talk about."

"How long have you been with Axel?" Samira asks as soon as we sit on our stools. She leans over and waves at the bartender. "We'll have two cappuccinos."

She turns to me, her eyes soft and warm. She's breathtaking. So confident in herself, the world, and her place in it. Her being with someone as handsome as Max makes much more sense than me being with three men like Kian, Ronan, and Axel.

"So, how long have you been with Axel?"

"Um, I'm not sure if we're together. It's still relatively new, but I've known him most of my life. Well, I haven't known him as such, but we've known of each other since we were in elementary school."

Samira laughs and takes a sip of her Coffee, "Let me guess. He noticed how hot you got, and now he's all on the prowl? What about the other guys?"

What about the other guys? I'm not sure how I'm going to answer her question. It's not like our relationship is something most people would understand. Sure, poly relationships are more prevalent in society than they were ten years ago, but it's still a hard conversation to have with someone. *Hey, I'm with Axel, but I'm also with his best friends. I fuck all of them, but they only bang each other and me. They're my boyfriends, but each other's too.*

A shadow lurks over me as the realization dawns that this will be a conversation I'll probably have with people for the rest of my life if I stay with the guys. But if I decide to leave, would they let me? They said they would, but they also said they wouldn't.

"It's complicated," I finally reply.

"You're fucking all of them, huh?"

"What? No! I mean, what? How do you know?"

"The deadly trio. That's how those three are known. They do everything together. Mind you, I've never heard of all three of them sharing one girl, but that doesn't shock me. If they all want you and if they brought you here for their meeting with Max and Alexie, they trust you, girl. To them, you're endgame. Men like ours have serious trust issues. It may not seem like a lot to you that they brought you here, but it's the world. Trust me"

"I'm probably a commodity to them."

Samira laughs. It sounds like chimes, pretty and sweet like she seems to be. She nods toward the table where all the men are sitting except for Mikhail. He's standing behind Max and Alexie. "Girl, those men can't concentrate on anything but you. Which in their line of work is a little stupid, so if you care about them even a little bit, you better make sure they know you're theirs, and that's where you wanna be. Trust me, these men rarely care about anyone or anything, but when they do, they are in it. They're dangerous, but they love hard. I'm blessed to have Maxim's love, and you, girl, seem to have bagged three of them."

I'm about to answer her, but a man leans between us, blocking my view of Samira. "Now, what's a pretty girl like you doing here without a man?"

"It's a little presumptuous of you to assume I'm here without someone," I respond.

He laughs as he trails a finger along my arm, making me flinch.

"You'd better crawl back to whatever hole you came out of before you find yourself buried six feet under," Samira says.

"No one asked you," the man snivels.

A scream escapes his mouth before he can say anything else. I don't know what's happening. All I see are the men surrounding him.

Kian's holding the man's head on the bar, broken glass and blood surrounding him. "No one asked me either, but I don't care. When you decide to fuck with other people's property, be prepared for other people to fuck with you."

"Kian, I think maybe you should let him go.

It's broad daylight," Max says, trying to talk Kian off the ledge.

"Let him do what he needs to do, Maxim. The man was rude to both of us."

Max's nostrils flare at Samira's words, and he lodges a pen right in the guy's eye.

Alexie laughs. "A little hypocritical, don't you think, Max?"

"Pull him into the back," Axel demands.

Kian lifts the man by his neck and drags him. We all follow down a corridor to a room in the back. Ronan opens the door, and Kian drops the man like he weighs nothing. The guy slumps to the floor, and fear washes over his face before he covers it, hoping to shield himself from whatever horror is about to be unleashed on him. One mangled eye oozes blood. He looks like he stepped out of a horror movie.

Axel methodically walks over to him, each step timed and ominous. He twirls a fork in one hand as his fingers graze the pointed ends. Axel doesn't say a word. He stabs the guy in the throat, and blood spurts out of his neck as the room fills with his deafening screams.

Axel moves closer to him, his blue eyes dark, his expression twisted and frightening.

"No one fucks with what's mine and lives to tell about it." He stabs him again, and again, and again. The blood is overwhelming.

Watching Axel like this is frightening and exhilarating all at once. That he has no issues defending me this way is a tremendous turn-on. I've had no one to fight my battles before, and the fact that these three men would without blinking, makes me feel wanted and special.

Axel gets up, wiping the bloody fork on a white napkin. Kian lifts his gun and blasts a bullet through the man's heart, causing his body to go lifeless and still.

Ronan grabs me in a fierce embrace. "You okay, Rabbit?"

I ponder his question. Am I okay? As fucked up as it is, this is the moment I have my answer. Standing in front of a dead body, surrounded by these three men, I realize without a shadow of a doubt that I belong to them, and they belong to me.

"I'm more than okay. I'm yours."

23

STELLA

"We need a favor," Axel says.

"What kind of favor?" I eye him suspiciously as I take a bite of the cheesecake he's placed in front of me.

In the last month, the guys have learned that sex and food are the best ways to get me to agree to anything they want. I still can't believe it's been over a month since I officially moved into the penthouse with them. And I have to admit I've never been happier.

"We got a job and wouldn't normally bring you into our shit, but we need a girl to get into this place, or we gotta get in a room with one."

A lump forms in my throat as I try to swallow it down. "What do you mean, you've got to be in a room with one?"

"My dad needs me to check out this new sex club. He thinks it's a competition and, well, you know him, he doesn't like much competition."

"You know I don't like y'all killing people."

Axel crosses his heart. "There won't be any killing." He grips my hips and pulls me to him. I can feel the strain of his erection against my stomach, causing me to groan. "There will be fucking. Lots and lots of fucking."

"You don't have to twist my arm."

"You got a room with the toys I requested, right?" I whisper in Axel's ear as we stand outside an elegant old hotel that's now a sex club.

Ronan squeezes my hand. "He got everything on your list. My only question is, who are you gonna use it on?"

I ignore Ronan and wrap my arms around Kian's waist, resting my head on his shoulder.

"Guess I've got my answer."

"As I told you earlier, you'll see when you see."

Ronan laughs and tugs at my ponytail. "All I know is I'm gonna have you on your fuckin' knees like the good girl you are."

The door of the club flings open. Kian grabs one hand while Ronan takes the other as the three of us walk in.

The place is classy, which surprises me. I'm not sure why, but I thought a sex club would be seedy, full of people on leashes and naked men and women having sex wherever possible. But this place looks like a fancy lounge; trendy, lush, and very proper-looking.

A pretty redhead approaches us like a maitre d at an expensive restaurant. "Hello, can I help you?"

Axel steps forward. "We've got a reservation. Axel Moretti."

She glances down at a ledger before flashing a smile with teeth so white they almost blind me. "Yes, Mr. Moretti, we've got your reservation right here." She hands him a key. "You'll be in room Twenty-Two. If you could take the elevator to the third floor, please."

The four of us walk into the elevator and wait until the door opens to the third floor.

"This place is nice. Nothing like I expected," I murmur.

Ronan laughs, his arm around my waist, bringing me closer to him. "The rich and famous, Rabbit. They pretend their depravity is fine, unlike the average person, because of the glitz and glam. Anything to deny they're like every other person on the planet.

We walk down the pristine corridor until we reach our room. Room Twenty-Two.

The guys let me walk in first. My eyes take in the white walls and the circle in the middle of the room. A giant California king bed sits in one corner with a menu, brand new toys, and cleaning solutions.

My eyes widen when I notice the Saint Andrew's Cross in the corner. The medieval structure looks out of place in the modern chic of the room. "I will not be on that torture device, right?'

Kian laughs, "Nah, we're not so much into that stuff." He kisses my neck. "But if you want to look at the table over there, you can pick out anything you want."

I take in all the toys on the table. Axel got what I asked, but he's also picked up some other things. Crops, whipes, vibrators, dildos, paddles, and rope. But what catches my eye is a large purple dildo and butt plugs.

"Get in the circle, Kitten," Axel demands.

"What?"

"You heard me, little sister. Be a good girl and do as your big brother asks. Get in the damn circle."

I moved to one end of the circle. Axel smiles, removing his suit jacket and crisp white dress shirt before stepping into the opposite side of the circle. He walks around, edging closer to me, and I step away, trying to avoid him.

"What are you doing, Kitten? Stay still," Axel growls.

This is a game for him. Axel likes to chase, and I like to be caught, but what gets me going is him making me submit. I'm not someone who will bend easily for him, which is what he needs. Axel doesn't want a submissive, he wants a challenge he can force into submission.

"Make me," I taunt.

Axel sports a lopsided, wolfish grin. "With pleasure, sis."

He leaps and is on me in an instant, his body covering mine like a blanket. I try to push him off me, but it's impossible. He's so much bigger. I claw his back, digging my nails in as I scrape them down his flesh.

He hisses but doesn't move. "Gotta try harder than that, Kitten."

His words enrage me. I glare at him and bite his shoulder. The metallic flavor of blood floods my mouth, but I keep biting harder, showing no mercy. Axel wants to play, then let's play. Let him get a taste of his own medicine.

Axel moans and digs his hard cock into me. I'm drenched. This whole exchange is a fucked-up aphrodisiac, an hors d'oeuvres leading up to the main event.

He loosens his grip on me, and I get on top of him. "You want it rough, Axel?" I punch him in the face and jump off him into the other end of the circle. "I'll give it to you rough."

"Oh, sis. You don't even know what you've started."

Before I can say anything, Axel barrels toward me, his fingers around my neck as he slams me into the wall without mercy. I feel the pain in my back, but the rush of endorphins is so high I don't care. This is Axel unleashed like he was in the forest.

He growls in my ear. "Ready to have your brother fuck your pussy again, Kitten? Not only am I going to destroy your cunt, but so are they. We're hungry, baby, and you're the main course."

I glance at Ronan and Kian. Predatory hunger lurks in their eyes. They're both naked, their large cocks at full mast, ready to join the fun. Kian grabs Ronan's dick, a smirk on his handsome face.

I struggle against Axel, and he laughs before crushing his lips to mine. His teeth dig into my bottom lip, pulling it toward him before he bites down. He doesn't care about the blood now flowing in our mouths. He pushes up against me, holding me immobile as his mouth explores mine with passion and need. The kiss is feral, uncontained, and bursting with heat. It's the kiss a man gives you when he's drowning, and only you can save him.

I'm lost in the moment, transfixed by Axel and the anticipation of what's coming.

24

KIAN

Doesn't she know that the more she struggles, the more we want her? Does she do it on purpose? Stella is a bad girl, trapped in the body of a good one, and there's nothing hotter.

She yelps as Axel tosses her on the bed by her throat. "How are you able to do that? I'm not a tiny girl."

Axel growls, stalking toward her. "I'm not a little bitch playing at being a man. I love your body, and I sure as fuck can handle it."

My fingers tug at Ronan's head as I direct him on my cock. It feels good. Ronan is a good cock sucker. He sucks dick like a champ. "Good boy. Take that cock in your mouth. Make me all nice and hard so I can pour all this cum in our girl's hot cunt."

"Fuck," Stella moans, bringing my attention back to her. She's spread eagle on the bed, Axel's head buried deep in her pussy as he tugs at the chain connected to nipple clamps.

Fuck.

My cock twitches in Ronan's mouth. I know those clamps are hurting her. I've seen the teeth on them. They will leave marks. "Make her scream, Axel. Pull those clamps harder."

Stella shrieks, and I ram my cock in Ronan's mouth, fucking it like it's her pussy. He gags as he swallows me deep, but I don't care. Ronan and Axel know the deal with me. I like it rough. It's the only way I can get off.

I stare down at Ronan. His eyes tear up, and his face turns red. "You look good with a cock in your mouth. Hold still while I fill it."

Ronan nods as my balls tighten, and I groan, spurting hot cum in his mouth. He opens up, displaying my cum. I grab his neck, pull him up to me, and kiss him, taking in my cum.

"Go fuck her mouth," I order. "Make it rough."

I sit back as I take in the show. Ronan slaps her face with his cock, and she winces. Ronan's well-endowed, and the slap he gave her wasn't gentle. Stella, like the good slut she is, opens wide for him. Her tongue sticks out, and she pulls away from the clamps, taking the pain like the perfect girl. She is desperate to take his dick in her mouth.

"Such a good girl, Rabbit," Ronan groans as he slowly pushes into her.

He lets her adjust for a minute before he pushes all the way down. Stella gags, but she doesn't stop. She keeps taking his cock like the good girl she is. I can't help my sense of pride at how well she handles us. She knows exactly when to push and when to submit, the perfect center to our universe.

Ronan pulls back, and drool falls from the corners of her mouth as she coughs. "You're doing so well, Rabbit." He grins before walking to the table full of sex toys. He grabs a pink vibrator, tossing it to Axel.

Stella moans as Axel places the vibrator on her clit while he thrusts into her cunt. She's losing all control, and I want to be in on the action. I want to make her scream with my dick in her, with all of us in here. I grab the lube and drain a silver butt plug with it.

The bed creaks as one of my knees hits the mattress. Axel lifts her legs, and I add more lube to her ass, messaging it into her back entrance. "I'm going to get you nice and ready, Sweet Girl, because I'm taking this ass tonight. We're gonna have cum leaking out of every hole."

"Oh, god," she moans as I push the plug into her ass. "Please, someone fuck my pussy."

Axel doesn't waste time. He pumps back into her while Ronan stands on the bed and lodges his cock in her mouth. I grab his balls, massaging them.

"Fuck, Kian, that feels good," he grunts.

I chuckle, pulling his cock out of Stella's mouth, pushing my mouth on him until I gag. The saliva floods my mouth as he pulls out. I turn to Stella and spit it in her mouth. "My pretty little slut. You've no idea how much I want you when you look like this. Our sexy fuck toy. Our perfect cum slut."

"Please, more. Give me—"

She doesn't get to finish her sentence because Ronan shoves his dick down her throat, gagging her.

"We don't need you to talk, Rabbit. We need you to lie there and take it. We want to use you. Be a good girl and say 'ah' for your brother and his friends like the good little whore we know you are."

I tug the plug from her ass with a pop before pushing my cock into her tight little asshole. She winces but soon relaxes and adjusts to my cock. "That's it, Sweet Girl. Bounce that sexy ass on my cock. Let Daddy know how much you want his cum in your asshole." I tug on her nipple clamps, my gaze on her bruised nipples. Her fingernails dig into the flesh of my thighs, but she doesn't protest at the pain.

"Fuck," Axel groans. "She's so tight when you're up her ass. I don't think I can hold off much longer."

"Hear that, Sweet Girl? Your brother is going to make your cunt leak with his cum."

25

RONAN

It's not lost on me that we're supposed to be checking this place out rather than fucking Stella like horny teenagers. But fuck, the girl has a hold on us. The way she moans on my dick every time Kian hurts her is so fucking hot. She's the only one who could do this. She gives us what we need, and we only work because of her.

"You want my cum, Rabbit?"

She nods at my question. Her mouth's too busy to form words.

Axel and Kian bounce her back and forth as I hold her head still, fucking her mouth. I want us to come together. To fill her and step back as she leaks it out of every hole.

Kian is pushing her harder, and the way he's grunting tells me he's close. Axel doesn't appear too far behind. "I'm gonna fuck your mouth hard, Rabbit. Keep your eyes on me, pretty girl. I want to see those chocolate-brown eyes when I unload into your mouth."

Axel's hands dig into my ass as he grunts, "Little sis, your pussy is gripping my cock so well. I'm coming in your sweet cunt, Kitten. I'm going to put a baby in you. You're gonna walk around with an enormous belly knowing you're carrying your big brother's baby."

Shit, Axel is filthy. Out of all of us, he's probably the best at dirty talk. The talk is so wrong and taboo that my cock twitches, and I hold still as I unload ropes of cum in Stella's mouth. "Don't swallow. I want to watch all your holes leak, Rabbit. We're gonna fill you with our cream."

"Fuck," Kian grunts, moving her up and down on him as he bites her flesh, sinking his teeth like a wild animal. "Fuck yes!" His body stills, and he holds Stella down, impaling her ass with his big dick.

I pull out and stand beside Axel, and our gazes linger on Stella's pussy. Kian's cock is still deep in her asshole. I touch her entrance, pushing Axel's leaking cum back into her pussy. "Keep my cum in your mouth, Rabbit. I'll let you know when to let it all leak out."

"God, her ass is so tight," Kian says as he gently lifts her off him, placing a pillow under her ass. "She milked my cock so quickly I felt like I was sixteen again."

Kian and Axel stand beside me. Stella is the main event of the show. "Push it all out, Rabbit. Let us know you're our good little cum slut."

Cum leaks from her ass, dripping down the pillow. Then she squeezes out what Axel left, but the best part is the two lines of cum dribbling from the sides of her mouth down her face and into her hair.

"Guess you're too spent to do what you planned, Sis. Better save it for an anniversary," Axel says before he licks my cum off her cheek and spits it back into her open mouth.

EPILOGUE

Five years later

STELLA

Best anniversary present ever. Five years too late, if you ask me. I stroke my cock and smile down at my guys.

I walk up to Ronan and pull his hair back before spitting on his face. "So pretty with my spit on your face. Such a good boy." Ronan smiles and winks at me. "Open your mouth and stick out your tongue."

Ronan doesn't hesitate. I gaze at his tongue sticking out like a dog desperate for a taste of meat.

I push the strap into his mouth, and his lips suction around it. I finally understand why guys like blow jobs so much. The control. I tug at his hair and push back as he gags on it. "Good boy, you're doing such a good job. Get that cock nice and wet for me."

I stare down at Axel. His cock is hard as nails, and a dollop of pre-cum hits the floor. "Touch your dick, Axel. It's okay to enjoy watching Ronan's throat being fucked. You want your sister's cock in your mouth too?" Axel visibly swallows the lump in his throat but says nothing. "Get the lube, Axel," I order, and he hops to his feet. "Hurry."

When Axel returns, I smirk—the same smirk he's given me over the years. "Get that ass ready, Bro. Make sure you lube it real good." His cock twitches as he pours an abundant amount of lube on his fingers. "Turn around, Axel. I want to see your fingers fucking your ass."

Axel rubs his lubed-up fingers along his crack before inserting one finger in his ass. "Be a good boy and stretch that ass nice and wide for me."

I've learned over the years that Axel loves his ass fucked. We've spent many nights with him fucking my pussy while one of the other guys rams his ass. He comes like a champ that way. It's one of my favorite things about my men—anything goes when it comes to sex. Whatever they do to me, they are more than willing to have done to them.

"Keep pumping your fingers, Bro." I turn to Kian. "Your turn, sweet boy. Show me how badly you want my cock in your ass."

Kian smiles and grabs my nipples, yanking hard. I nod, letting him know it's okay because this is what he needs. "It's okay, baby. Go get it." Causing me pain adds to Kian's pleasure.

He picks up the small knife on the night-stand and brings the sharp end to my right tit. He digs in the blade, and blood trickles from my breast. Kian latches on, lapping it up. His fingers move back to my nipples, causing my pain and his pleasure.

"Ronan, get Kian nice and ready for my cock," I demand

Ronan takes the lube from Kian and pours it on his lower back, between his ass cheeks. His fingers slowly disappear into Kian's asshole. "You ready for me, Kian? Ready for my big dick in your ass? You gonna be a good boy for me?"

Kian growls at me but bends over, pulling his ass apart. Before gliding it up and down his crack, I pour some of the lube on the strap-on. "I'm gonna make you my little bitch, Kian. I'm gonna pound your ass so hard. You ready to be mommy's good boy?"

"Hope you enjoy this, Sweet Girl," Kian says through gritted teeth. His gaze takes me in hungrily. A look passes between us that promises whatever I do to him tonight, he'll take out on me tomorrow. Kian has never bottomed for the guys. The fact he's agreed to do it for me is an enormous concession. He's doing it out of love, to show me I'm safe, that I'm the one he needs and wants.

I bend over and whisper in Kian's ear, "You're going to fuck Ronan while I fuck you."

Kian smirks at me before grabbing Ronan by the throat and bending him over. He pushes into Ronan slowly and adjusts himself. Kian is bent over, his ass presented to me.

I tug his hair back. "Fuck him good for me, sweet boy. Show him the same pleasure I'm going to show you." I push into Kian slowly, and he groans. "Feels good to be filled by a nice cock, doesn't it?"

"Fuck," Kian groans, his hand holding onto Ronan as I fuck him slowly.

Calloused hands grab onto my waist, fingers digging into my flesh as cold liquid slides into my ass, followed by a hand. "I'm gonna take your ass while you take his, Kitten." The head of Axel's cock pushes into me slowly before he's in me all the way. Even with the lube, it hurts. It always hurts at first with these three. They aren't exactly small.

"Kitten," Axel whispers in my ear. "You're so fuckin' hot."

I move quicker in Kian, causing my ass to fuck Axel while I attack Kian's ass with my cock. Power surges through me as I take him, own him, make him mine. I move my hand to his ass and squeeze it.

He jerks as I slap his ass. "You look so good taking my cock. Such a good boy."

Axel chuckles in my ear. "He's going to make you pay for this later."

I turn my head to Axel and smile. "Oh, I'm well aware. I'm looking forward to it."

Ronan is the first one to come, He's tugging his cock, and he grunts as his cum hits the floor. "Fuck," he groans. He tries to pull away, but Kian's hands hold him still.

"You're not going anywhere, Ronan. Not until I empty my hot load into your ass."

"Fuck," Axel whispers in my ear. "If he keeps talking like that, I'm gonna cum in your sweet ass earlier than I want. Why the fuck is this so hot?"

"You still don't know you're a depraved fuck, huh, big brother?"

"No, Kitten, I've known for a long time. But I save most of my depravity for you. Didn't realize it extended to those two."

"Fill my ass, Axel. I know you want to see your cum leaking out of me."

Axel stiffens inside me, holding me still. A

smirk forms on my face as his cum floods my ass. "Once you're done with Kian, I'm gonna eat your sweet cunt until you scream my name."

I fuck Kian harder, pushing both him and Ronan onto the bed. He holds on to Ronan as Ronan fists the cover. "Be a good boy and come for me!" I yell.

"Oh, dear god," he grunts before his whole body stiffens, and he falls on top of Ronan.

Hands grip my hips, pulling me out of Kian before removing the strap-on. Axel grabs my neck, pushing me onto the bed.

"Spread them, slut," Axel demands. But he doesn't give me time to obey. His hand roams up my legs, gripping my knees before moving my legs apart. I'm there, spread eagle, exposed to the three men I love more than anything and who love me more than their next breath. "Fuckin beautiful."

Axel slaps my pussy, "Who do you belong to?"

"To the three of you."

Kian bites my nipple before asking, "Who loves you?"

"The three of you."

Kian pulls my hair, forcing my eyes on his. “Who do you love?’

“The three of you.”

Then End

Made in United States
Orlando, FL
16 July 2022

19852445R00100